# RICH MAN, POOR MAN,
# BEGGARMAN, THIEF

# Rich Man, Poor Man, Beggarman, Thief

Folk Tales from Around the World

Marcus Crouch

*Illustrated by William Stobbs*

Oxford University Press

OXFORD TORONTO MELBOURNE

Oxford University Press, Walton Street, Oxford OX2 6DP

*Oxford London*
*New York Toronto Melbourne Auckland*
*Kuala Lumpur Singapore Hong Kong Tokyo*
*Delhi Bombay Calcutta Madras Karachi*
*Nairobi Dar es Salaam Cape Town*

and associated companies in
*Beirut Berlin Ibadan Mexico City Nicosia*

*Oxford* is a trade mark of Oxford University Press

Text © Marcus Crouch 1985
Illustrations © William Stobbs 1985
First published 1985

ISBN 0 19 278116 2

*British Library Cataloguing in Publication Data*
Crouch, Marcus
  Rich Man, Poor Man, Beggarman, Thief
  I. Title   II. Stobbs, William
  823'.914[J]   PZ7

ISBN 0-19-278111-1

Typeset by Tradespools Limited, Frome, Somerset
Printed in Great Britain by Butler and Tanner Ltd, Frome, Somerset

# CONTENTS

*For Grace Hallworth*

ENGLAND

# MR AND MRS VINEGAR

MR AND MRS Vinegar lived very happily together. And where do you think they lived? In a vinegar bottle of course; where else?

One day Mrs Vinegar decided to give her home a good cleaning. She was swishing away with her broom—swish-swash—and the broom hit the wall very hard. There was a loud crash, the glass cracked from roof to floor, and down came the house in a heap of sharp splinters.

Mrs Vinegar ran to tell her husband the bad news. He looked at the ruins and said,

1

'Don't fret, my love. See, there is our front door, just as good as new. Let us take that and go out into the world to find what it has to offer.'

So they went. Mr Vinegar carried the door slung over his back, and Mrs Vinegar carried her broom—because you never know when you may find something to clean. They reached a forest at nightfall. How tired they were! Mr Vinegar said, 'We must find somewhere to sleep. I will climb up this tree and take the door with me. If I lay it between two branches it will make a fine floor for our bedroom, and we can sleep there quite safely.' So that is what they did.

In the night they were awakened by a great noise. A gang of robbers had settled down under their tree, sharing out the spoils of their latest crime. They were shouting and drinking and firing their weapons. Mr Vinegar was filled with terror, so much that he shook in every limb. The door slipped from the branch and went clattering down on top of the robbers. They were scared out of their wits and went running this way and that through the forest.

Mr and Mrs Vinegar stayed up the tree until daybreak in case the wicked men came back. Then they climbed down and picked up their door. What do you think was underneath it? Why, the robbers' loot, a hundred pounds in bright gold.

Weren't Mr and Mrs Vinegar pleased with their good luck! 'Our fortune's made,' cried Mr Vinegar. 'Yes,' said Mrs Vinegar, 'but we must spend it wisely. I know. Here is forty pounds. You must go to the fair today and buy a cow. Then I can make butter and cheese, and you will sell them in the market. That way we shall live very well and have no more worries.'

So Mr Vinegar took the money and went off to the fair.

He walked up and down, looking closely at all the animals. There was one cow; oh, she was a beauty and no mistake, bright red with a pair of horns on top and a set of udders below, promising a supply of rich creamy milk. 'Ah!' said Mr Vinegar, 'if that were my cow, there would be no happier man on earth.' And he went to the owner and offered him forty golden pounds. 'Done,' said the man, after a little argument, and Mr Vinegar got a rope and led his cow away in triumph.

In a corner of the fair he noticed a man playing the bagpipes. He was a fat, happy man, and he had people all around him dropping pennies in his hat. 'Now there's a way to make a living,' said Mr Vinegar. 'If I had those bagpipes, there would be no happier man on earth.' When the man put down his pipes for a rest Mr Vinegar went to him. 'Good day to you, friend,' he said. 'Those are fine pipes you have there. Would you think of parting with them?' 'I might,' said the man, 'if the price was right. Now I wouldn't say no to that cow of yours.' 'Done,' said Mr Vinegar, and he handed over the cow and picked up the bagpipes.

'Now to earn some money,' said Mr Vinegar. He tucked the pipes under his arm, and all the people crowded around to hear his music. But Mr Vinegar

had never played bagpipes, or any other pipes, in all his life, and he had no idea how to start. All he could do was make some very loud and rude noises. Instead of pennies, stones and rubbish were showered on him and he had to run for his life.

Playing the bagpipes, however badly, was hard on the fingers, and Mr Vinegar's hands felt so cold he could hardly bear them. As he was leaving the fairground he noticed a man with a pair of thick, warm gloves on. 'I'm so cold,' said Mr Vinegar. 'Oh, if I had those gloves, there would be no happier man on earth.' He went up to the man and said, 'That's a good pair of gloves you've got there.' 'Why, yes,' said the man. 'My hands are so warm; it might be midsummer and not getting on for Christmas.' 'I don't suppose,' said Mr Vinegar, 'that you would think of parting with them?' 'Perhaps I would and perhaps I wouldn't,' said the man. 'It depends on the price. Now, if you were to offer those bagpipes I might agree.' 'Done,' said Mr Vinegar, and so they made the exchange.

Mr Vinegar started for home, wearing his gloves and feeling warm and happy. But the way was long and he got more and more tired. Down the road came a man, swinging a fine stick. 'Ah,' said Mr Vinegar, 'that's the way to walk without tiring. If I had a stick like that, there would be no happier man on earth.' He called out to the man: 'Good day to you, friend. That's a fine stick you have there. Would you think of parting with it?' 'Well,' said the man, 'that stick of mine is an old friend. He's kept me company for many a mile, and I like him better

5

than a brother. Still, it's good to please a friend when you meet him on the highway. Here, take the stick and give me those gloves you are wearing.' 'Done,' said Mr Vinegar.

Mr Vinegar went on his way, swinging his stick and whistling happily. The road passed through a wood which was full of birds and they were all singing. It seemed to Mr Vinegar that what they were singing made words and those words were addressed to him. They sang:

> '*Silly old Vinegar,*
> *Got him a fortune,*
> *Went to the fair*
> *And bought a fine cow.*
> *Swopped her for bagpipes,*
> *Gloves and a walking-stick.*
> *Forty pounds down*
> *And nothing to show.'*

Mr Vinegar was so angry that he threw his stick up into the trees, where it missed the birds and got stuck beyond his reach. So he went home, without his money, without the cow or the bagpipes or the gloves or even the walking-stick. But Mrs Vinegar gave him a warm welcome with her broom. She whacked and banged him till he didn't know whether he was coming or going, upside or down.

ICELAND

# THE TROLL IN LOVE

THORSTEIN was a good fisherman. He worked hard too, going out every day in his boat, never mind how bad the weather. Yet little good came of all his hard work because all the profits of his fishing were spent on his two elder daughters, silly spoiled girls who loved to dress in fine clothes and hang ornaments on themselves. He had another daughter too called Helga, who got nothing but the leavings and these weren't many. She did all the dirty work and had no bed but the hearth where she kept warm among the ashes.

One day Thorstein was out at sea when a great storm arose, and he had his work cut out to keep the boat right side up. Then a hand came out of the sea and lifted his boat right out of the water. It belonged to a troll. This jolly fellow promised to drag him and his boat down to the bed of the sea unless he gave up one of his daughters.

Well, what was a man to do? He had to tell the troll he should have the eldest girl that very same day. The troll was satisfied, the sea calmed down, and Thorstein sailed home as fast as he could.

He went in and said nothing to anyone. But when he was in the middle of his supper there was a sudden flurry of rain on the window, and looking out he saw the troll outside.

'Hey, eldest daughter,' said the fisherman, 'I left my knife in the boat. Run and get it.'

She went outside and the troll grabbed her. 'Give us a kiss, lass,' he grunted, but she would do nothing but scream. So he just threw her over his shoulder and went off with her.

'That's a pity,' thought the fisherman, 'but I've still got another daughter—two if you count Helga.' So he went out fishing as usual next day. Sure enough, there was another storm, and the troll appeared, as ugly as ever.

'Give me another daughter or you will find what the sea tastes like.'

Thorstein had to agree, and the troll allowed him to sail home. That evening he told his second daughter to go to the boat and fetch his sea-boots, and the troll caught her too. She wouldn't kiss him, not she, and he took her away kicking and yelling.

Still the troll was not satisfied. He picked up the boat next day, and the fisherman had to promise to give him his last daughter. The same thing happened. Thorstein sent Helga to get his cap from the boat, and there stood the troll, looking bigger and uglier than ever.

'Give us a kiss, lass,' he said in his harsh voice that sounded like a hundred thunderclaps.

'Surely,' said Helga, and she gave him a big kiss, and hugged as much of him as she could reach. Then the troll picked her up and took her off to his home, which was in a large damp cave.

'Cook my supper,' said the troll, and she did that so well that the troll was satisfied. He went away to his sleeping place, and Helga looked around the cave. In a dark passage she found her two sisters. They were starving, for, having refused to cook for the troll, they had been given no food for themselves, and they were scared half out of their wits. She ran and got them some food and cheered them as best she could.

Next day the troll said to Helga: 'You seem a likely lass. Will you marry me?'

'Why not?' she said. So he began to make preparations for the wedding. Helga was set to clean out the cave, while he went away to find some food. He came back with a cow—stolen of course— and this he killed and cut up.

'You won't need all that meat,' said Helga. 'Can't you spare some for my father and mother? Just enough to fill this sack.'

9

'All right,' said the troll, and he set aside a good slab of meat.

Next day Helga told her sisters to climb into the sack. Then she called the troll and asked him to take it to her father's house. 'Don't look inside, whatever you do,' she said, 'or you will bring bad luck on yourself.'

The troll took the sack. It seemed mighty heavy and he was sore tempted to peep inside. 'Shall I? Shan't I?' he said to himself. But the thought of Helga's warning and the fire in her eyes when she said it were enough to scare him, for all his size and strength, and he staggered on with his burden and left it outside the cottage.

The wedding day dawned. The troll told Helga to get the cave ready while he went to fetch the guests. Helga decorated the cave and laid the table. Then she picked out a big log of wood from the pile stacked ready by the fire, and dressed it up in her wedding clothes. Set upright it looked just like a bride.

Helga then found some old rags in the back of the cave and dressed herself in them. She rubbed soot from the fire into her face and arms until she looked like a grubby old woman. She was now ready to go home.

On the way she met the troll and his wedding guests. My, they were a strange crowd, monsters of all shapes and sizes, and all riding great horses that were no more than skin and bone. They were making a terrible noise. The troll saw Helga and bellowed: 'Hey there, old woman. Did you come past my cave? And was the feast ready and the bride dressed?'

'Yes,' said Helga in a creaky old woman's voice.

'Come on, lads,' said the troll, and they all raced on to the cave.

There stood the bride, dressed in all her finery.

'Are you ready, then?' said the troll.

Not a word replied the log.

'What are we waiting for?' said the troll.

Still the log took no notice of him. He was getting impatient, and he spoke sharply to his bride. Still she gave him back not one single word. At last he lost his temper and gave the log a slap in the face, and it fell over and landed on his foot.

'You fool, you've killed her,' shouted some of the guests.

'It's not his fault, she drove him to it,' said others. And in no time at all they were all taking sides and arguing. Words led to actions, and a tremendous fight began. They picked up trees and rocks to throw at one another, and when the fight finished the troll and all his guests were stretched out dead.

Meanwhile Helga went home. There she found her sisters, safely recovered, and now ready to treat their young sister much better than they had ever done. After a few days she went back to the cave, and in a far corner she found the troll's treasure hoard of gold and precious stones. So that was all right.

NORWAY

# THE LAD WITH SIX FRIENDS

THERE were three brothers. The two elder brothers had good names straight out of the Bible—Peter and Paul they were called—but the youngest, well, dear knows what he was christened because he was known to everyone as Ashy. That's because he was for ever messing about with the fire, poking and prodding it and getting covered in ashes.

It was Sunday, and Ashy went to church. He came home very excited. 'Guess what,' he said. 'The king wants a ship that will go

as well on land as on sea, and he will give half his
kingdom and his daughter as well to anyone who
can build it. Parson read it out in church, so it must
be true.'

Peter thought he would have a go. He got his
mother to pack up a sack of food, and he took his
axe and went off to the woods. On the way he
passed a little bent old man.

'Where are you going in such a hurry, young
lad?' said the man.

'I'm going to the woods to make a feeding-
trough for my dad. He refuses to eat off the table
like the rest of us.'

'Then trough is what it will turn out,' said the
old man. 'What have you got in your sack?'

'Just a load of cow-dung.'

'Dung is what it is,' said the man.

Peter went on, and he swung his axe among the
oak trees. He chopped and cut with all his might,
but, do you know?—all he could make were
troughs, dozens of them, and not one was anything
like a ship. In the end, what with all the hard work
and the vexation, he came over mighty hungry. So
he opened his sack, and what do you think was in
it? Yes, it was cow-dung! He couldn't eat that, so he
went home in a temper.

Next day Paul decided to try his hand at ship-
building. He took his axe and a sack full of food,
and strode off to the woods. He too met the old bent
man.

'Where are you going?' asked the man.

'I'm off to the woods. Our sow has had a litter,

and I am going to make a trough for the piglets.'

'Pig-trough it is,' said the man. 'And what's in the sack?'

'Pig-muck.'

'Pig-muck it is then.'

So Paul went to the woods, but work as hard as he might he could make nothing but pig-troughs. It made him mad, especially as they didn't keep a single pig at home. In the end he gave up trying and sat down to have some food. But the sack was full to the brim with pig-muck. So Paul went home.

Next morning Ashy said: 'Perhaps I can build the king a ship. Can I have some food for the day?'

'That's likely,' said his mother. 'You're more likely to fall over your own feet and chop off your head with your axe. No food for you.'

Ashy had a look around when his mother was out of the house, and he found some bits of stale bread and half a pint of very sour beer. He put these in his sack, took up his axe, and wandered off to the woods.

On the way he came upon a bent old man.

'Good day, lad,' said the man. 'And where are you off to this bright morning?'

'I'm going to the woods to make a ship that goes on land and water, and then the king will give me half his kingdom and his daughter into the bargain.'

'And what do you have in that sack?'

'Nothing much,' said Ashy. 'Just a few bits of food to last the day.'

'Will you share it with me?' said the old man.

'Gladly, for what it is worth. But you won't get fat on it.'

So they went to the woods and sat down and ate together. Then the old man said: 'Right! Now this is what you must do. Just cut one chip out of that oak tree, and then put it back where it came from. When that is done, you can lie back and take a bit of a rest.'

Ashy did as he was told, and very soon he was dozing, yet in his sleep he seemed to hear a great noise of hammering and sawing. When he awoke, there was a ship, finished to the last nail.

'There she is,' said the old man. 'She will sail on land and water. Off you go, and don't forget to give a lift to anyone you meet on the way.'

Ashy climbed aboard, and the ship went beautifully.

Before long he came up to a man lying by the road, chewing lumps of stone.

'That's a fine ship,' said the man. 'May I sail in her?'

'Jump aboard,' said Ashy. 'But tell me, why do you chew stone?'

'I'm so hungry,' said the man. 'I just can't get enough meat to eat, and the stone helps to fill the space in my belly.'

They sailed on, and saw a man sitting by the road sucking the bung of a beer-barrel.

'Let me sail in your ship, captain,' he shouted.

'Get in,' said Ashy. 'But what are you doing with that bung?'

'Oh, I've got such a thirst. I've drunk all the beer

16

I can get my tongue round, so now I just have to make do with the bung.'

The next man they met was lying flat with his ear to the ground.

'Hallo, there,' he called. 'May I join you?'

'Surely,' said Ashy. 'But you must tell me, what are you doing with your ear to the ground?'

'Just listening to the grass growing. I've got good hearing.'

Ashy and his three new friends sailed on. They saw a man standing on a hill aiming a gun into the air. He shouted: 'Give me a ride in your ship.'

'Come along,' said Ashy. 'But why are you aiming your gun at nothing at all?'

'I have very good sight. I was aiming at a hare running along the lip of the world.'

The next man they met was hopping along on one foot with a huge stone tied to the other. 'Just what I wanted,' he said. 'I would like to sail in your ship.'

'We will enjoy your company,' said Ashy. 'But must you bring that great rock with you?'

'My trouble is that I run so fast, if I didn't tie myself down I'd run over the edge of the world in less than five minutes.'

Now Ashy had five companions on his ship. There was just one still to come. They soon saw him, standing with one hand pressed tightly against his mouth. He found it difficult to talk like this, but he waved his other hand to show that he wanted a lift.

'Come aboard,' said Ashy. 'Is there anything

wrong with your mouth?'

The man mumbled, 'I have got seven summers and fifteen winters tucked away inside me. If I opened my mouth wide they would all fall out at once and then there would be trouble.'

So they sailed on, Ashy and his six friends, until they came to the king's palace. Ashy moored his ship in the yard, and went to ask the king for his reward.

Well, the king looked at Ashy. The lad looked a proper mess, what with the ashes and the sawdust from ship-building and the dust of his long voyage overland. His clothes were ragged too. In fact he looked not at all like the bridegroom a king would choose for his daughter, let alone the ruler of half a kingdom.

'You will have to do more than this to earn your reward,' said the king. 'In my storehouse there are three hundred barrels of beef. Clear it out in twenty-four hours and the princess is yours.'

'I'll do my best,' said Ashy. 'I've got six friends with me. Can they help?'

'It'll do no harm.' And the king added quietly to himself: 'And no good neither!'

Ashy called for the man who chewed stone, and they went together to the storehouse. The man got busy on those barrels, and in half the time he had eaten the lot, all but six joints of meat which he saved for his shipmates' supper.

'The job's done,' said Ashy to the king. 'Now where's that princess?'

'Not so fast,' said the king. 'I have another little

task for you. In the cellar there are three hundred barrels of beer. I want them emptied right away. You have got twenty-four hours.'

Ashy called the man who sucked the bung and they went into the cellar. It took that man barely six hours to drink the beer—leaving just six pints for his companions—and even after that he was still thirsty.

'I have done that little job,' said Ashy to the king. 'It's time you kept your promise.'

'Not just yet,' said the king. 'The princess is waiting for her morning tea. Fetch me the water for it from the well at the world's end. I'll give you just ten minutes.'

'Get rid of that weight on your foot,' said Ashy to the runner. 'You will need both legs for this race.' So the runner got a pail, kicked off his weight, and in a flash he was out of sight.

The minutes went by and he didn't come back. Ashy waited five minutes, then six, then seven. Still no runner and no water.

Ashy called for the man with sharp hearing. 'Can you hear what Runner is up to?'

'The silly fellow has gone to sleep,' said Big-Ears. 'I can hear him snoring.'

'Here, Shooter,' said Ashy. 'Take careful aim and wake up that lazy Runner. Don't damage him, or he won't be able to run home.'

Shooter took aim and fired, and his bullet killed a fly that was standing on Runner's nose. Runner woke up with a start, grabbed the pail of water, and ran back at top speed. Ashy took the pail and handed it to the king. There was just half a minute still to go.

'Make the princess's tea and tell her to put on her wedding dress.'

The king stared at Ashy. He still looked very grubby.

'You need a bath first,' he said

So Ashy and his six friends went into the bath-house, and the king locked the door behind them. Then he ordered the fires that heated the bath to be lit. Wood was piled on the fire, and it got so hot that you could have melted iron inside.

Ashy said: 'It's getting warm. It is time that our sixth friend did some work. Just let out a half-dozen winters.' And as the sixth man took away his hand from his mouth, cold air flooded the bath-house. For a time it was quite comfortable, but towards dawn the air got chilly. Then the sixth man let out a couple of summers, and that made it just right.

In the morning they heard the king unlocking the door. 'Now let us have two more winters and let him have them right in the face,' said Ashy. So when the king opened the door, hoping to find all seven men cooked to cinders, he caught an icy blast that turned his nose into an icicle.

'What about that wedding?' said Ashy.

'The sooner the better,' gasped the king.

So they had it there and then, and a merry time they had, Ashy and the princess and the six useful friends. As for the king, he never said a word all day; he was too busy trying to thaw out his nose.

CZECHOSLOVAKIA

# CLEVER AND LUCKY

CLEVER was sitting at his ease one day, thinking about how very wise he was. Up came Lucky. 'Shove up! I want to sit down too.'

'Why should I? You're no better than me.'

'That's what you think,' said Lucky. 'I judge people by what they can do. Let's have a contest. Do you see that poor fellow down there, toiling away at the plough? I bet you can't do more for him than I can. If you can I'll gladly let you have your seat in peace, and bother you no more.'

'Agreed,' said Clever, and he went down and crept right inside the young peasant. At once the boy thought: 'What am I doing here, wasting my life? I can do better than this.'

He left the plough lying in the furrow and went home. 'I'm tired of this life, Dad,' he said. 'I want to be a gardener.'

'You must be crazy,' said his father. 'We've always been ploughmen, my father, and his father, and his, as far back as you can think, and ploughmen we always will be. But if you don't like work, you are no use to me. Be off with you. Your brother can do your work, and he will have the farm and everything when I'm gone.'

'Who cares about that?' said the lad. He packed a bag, and went off to the city, and got himself a job working in the king's garden. The chief gardener found him a quick learner. In fact he knew everything before the gardener could teach him, and very soon he was doing everything his own way and taking no notice of his orders. The old gardener was inclined to be annoyed at this, but he saw how well the garden was prospering under the younger man's care, so he didn't complain. 'You are a clever lad,' he said.

The garden was now so beautiful that the king took to walking in it every day. Sometimes he brought the queen with him, and sometimes the princess.

The princess was young and very beautiful, but ever since she was a child she had been dumb. This was a great sorrow to her father, and he made it known that whoever cured the princess should have her for his wife.

There was no lack of men—princes and kings and great lords—to try their luck, but nothing ever came of their efforts. The princess just smiled sweetly at them but spoke never a word.

'Here's my chance,' said the young gardener to himself. 'I've got more brains in my left elbow than all these high-born fools put together. I'll see what I can do.'

He went to the palace and told them his business, and they led him to the princess's room. There she sat, as pretty as any picture, cuddling the little dog which was her favourite companion. The gardener took no notice at all of the princess. Instead he addressed himself to the dog and said:

'Excuse me, Your Dogship. I am told you are mighty clever. I would be obliged for your advice. I was travelling with two friends, a carver of wood, a tailor, and myself, a gardener. When night fell we were in the forest, and wolves were howling nearby. We lit a fire, and agreed to take turns in keeping watch. The carver took the first watch. He got bored doing nothing, so he picked a log out of the fire and carved the figure of a girl out of it.

'When it was time he woke the tailor. "Whatever is that?" asked the tailor. "Oh, I had time on my hands, so I carved this girl. Why don't you make a dress for her?" And the tailor did just that.

'The tailor woke me at the right time, and I asked him what he had been doing. He showed me the wooden girl in her new dress. "You can pass the time teaching her to talk," he said. Well, I worked away through the rest of the night, and by morning she could speak pretty well. Then the three of us had an argument. Each of us wanted the girl, for each of us had put something into making her what she was.

'Now, My Lord Dog, what I want to know is this; which of the three has the best right to the girl?'

The dog said not a word—didn't even bark. But the princess spoke, and said: 'You. A girl is nothing without speech. The body and the clothes are worthless unless they are brought to life by words. You gave her the best gift, for you gave her life, and she is yours.'

'You have spoken the truth,' said the gardener. 'I have given you speech, and you are mine.'

'That is all very well,' said one of the king's ministers. 'You are a clever fellow, and no doubt His Majesty will give you a rich reward for what you have done, but you cannot marry a princess. Clever or not, you are base-born, a nothing. The princess must marry a nobleman at the very least.'

'Quite right,' said the king. 'Here, fellow. You shall have a thousand pounds and our royal thanks. You cannot hope for more than that.'

'I will have the princess,' said the young man. 'The king gave his royal word, and the king's word is law. The king has no choice; he must give me his daughter.'

'Treason!' shouted everybody. 'No one tells

the king what he must do. You are a traitor, and traitors must die.'

'Take him away,' said the king. 'If he won't see reason, the lad must die.'

So they took the gardener away to the place of execution.

'See where your cleverness has led to,' whispered Lucky to Clever. 'Now it is my turn.'

So Clever came out of the gardener and Lucky took his place. He was only just in time. The executioner lifted his axe and gave one mighty swing. The axe missed the gardener and broke in two pieces on the side of the scaffold. At that moment a messenger rode up, waving a flag and blowing a trumpet. The king had changed his mind!

The princess had been talking to him. She had pointed out that the gardener had spoken only the truth; the king's word was law. If the gardener was not noble enough to marry a princess, why then, the king must make him a nobleman. It was quite simple.

So they brought back the gardener. He knelt down and the king said: 'Arise, Prince Gardener!' Then everyone was happy.

Just as the new prince and his princess were driving away after their wedding, Clever saw Lucky walking down the road. At once he turned aside, pretending that he had not seen him. Since then, Clever and Lucky have taken care not to be found in the same company, for they just don't mix.

RUSSIA

# WHOSE FOAL?

T HEY were twin brothers, but what a difference between them! One never had two pennies to jingle in his pocket; the other must have kept a magnet in his purse, because money seemed to flow into it. But still he wanted more.

The brothers went on a journey together. At night they put up at an inn and tied their horses to the rail outside, first the rich man's splendid gelding, then his cart, last the poor brother's tired old mare. During the night the mare dropped her foal, and by chance the young one rolled under the cart. Next morning the rich man shook his brother out of his sleep and said: 'Get up. Come and see a miracle. My cart has borne a foal during the night.'

'That's a pretty story,' said the poor man. 'When did you ever hear of a cart having a foal? My mare bore that foal, and well you know it. The foal is mine.'

'If it were the mare's foal, surely it would be lying at its mother's side.'

They argued the matter for a long time and came to no agreement. At last they took their quarrel to the law court. The wise judge listened carefully to both sides but seemed inclined to favour the rich man. Perhaps he was impressed by the strength of his case; it was just possible that he was thinking about the purse of money that the rich man had quietly slipped into his wide judge's sleeve.

The case aroused some interest in the country and even the Tsar came to hear of it. He was amused and decided to hear the argument himself. Then he said: 'I will ask you a riddle and judge you by your replies. Listen carefully. What is the strongest and fastest thing in the world? What is the fattest? What the softest? And what the loveliest?' Then he sent them away with orders to come back with their answers in three days' time.

Riddles meant nothing to the rich man; he had always spent all his time thinking up new ways of cheating his neighbours. So he took his problem to his old grandmother. She was known to be a wise woman. She had no difficulty with the riddles. 'The strongest and fastest thing must be my son's mare: she runs like the wind. Nothing could be fatter than our old sow: she has eaten so much that her four legs can barely carry her. As for the softest thing, that's my daughter's hair, no doubt about that. And the loveliest thing? That's my newest great-grandson Ivan for sure: the sweet poppet he is!'

The rich man was well pleased with these answers.

As for his poor brother, he went home in a gloomy mood; he had never been able to guess riddles. His little daughter—just seven years old—ran to meet him.

'Why are you so sad, my father?'

'The Tsar has set me a riddle and I don't know the answer.'

'Tell me the riddle, father.'

'What is the strongest and fastest thing in the world, what the fattest, what the softest, and what the loveliest?'

'That's easy. Go to the Tsar and tell him: the strongest and fastest thing in the world is the wind; the fattest thing is the earth which feeds every living thing; the softest is the hand—however hard the ground you lie on you may rest your head on your hand and sleep deeply; and the loveliest thing of all is sleep.'

The two brothers knelt before the Tsar. He listened to their answers. Then to the rich man he said shortly: 'You are a fool.' And to the poor man:

'Are these your own answers, or did someone else give them to you?'

The man said: 'I have a daughter just seven years old and she told me what to say.'

'That is a clever girl. Let me see how clever she is.' The Tsar took a thread of silk and gave it to the man. 'Tell her I want an embroidered scarf made from this. Bring it in the morning or your life will pay for your failure.'

Home went the poor man, more miserable than ever. The little girl laughed when she heard what she had to do. She broke a twig off a tree and gave it to her father. 'Give this to the Tsar. Tell him to have a loom made out of it. When that is ready I will weave my scarf on it.'

The Tsar listened to this answer. He neither smiled nor frowned. He went to the kitchen for a hundred eggs and gave them to the man. 'Tell your daughter she is to hatch a hundred chicks. Bring them here tomorrow morning.'

The child laughed even more merrily at this order. She took the eggs and cooked them, and she and her father feasted at dinner and supper too. 'Tell the king this,' she said, 'and make sure you get the words just right. The chicks need one-day grain for their feed. The Tsar must have a field ploughed, and the seed sown and harvested, all in a single day. Otherwise those poor chicks will starve.'

The Tsar nodded his head when he heard this answer. 'You have a clever child,' he said. 'I will talk to her myself. Tell her to come to me tomorrow. She will come neither on foot nor on horseback, neither clothed nor naked, and she must bring me, yet not bring me, a present.'

The daughter smiled when she heard what she had to do. To her father she said: 'You must help me. I need a live hare and a live pigeon. See to it.' And this he did.

Early next morning the little girl took off all her clothes and wrapped herself in a fishing-net. She held the pigeon in one hand, and she climbed on the hare's back. In this fashion she went to the palace. There stood the Tsar. The girl jumped down from the hare and gave it a smack, so that it trotted off. She bowed low before the Tsar, saying: 'Greetings, Your Most Exalted Highness! I bring you a gift.' She handed him the pigeon. He put out his hand to take it, but as she let go the bird shot into the air and away to the safety of the woods. 'Oh dear!' said the child. 'You never got your present.'

'You are a clever little girl,' said the Tsar. 'You have done what I asked. Now I have one last question. Your father is a very poor man. What do you live on?'

'We do very well,' said the child. 'Father catches plenty of fish in the trees.'

'O foolish child,' said the Tsar. 'Who ever heard of fish living in trees?'

'O wise Tsar,' said the little girl. 'Who ever heard of carts having foals? In my part of the country only mares have foals.'

So the Tsar gave judgment in favour of the poor man who took home his little foal with great satisfaction. As for the little girl, the Tsar took her

into his own household, and when she was old enough he married her to his only son. The land had never known so wise a princess.

ROMANIA

# GOLDEN TWINS

THE youngest son of a great nobleman was coming back from the wars. As he rode through a village he saw three girls at work outside their cottage. They were talking together, and when he got up to them they all broke into peals of laughter.

'Won't you share your joke with me?' he said.

The eldest girl blushed and said: 'I was just saying that if the young man riding by were to marry me I would make him a beautiful home with nothing but my spindle and a skein of flax.'

'And I,' said the second, 'was saying that if the young man riding by were to marry me I would feed him and his family with only a handful of meal.'

The youngest girl said: 'I was saying that if the young man riding by were to marry me I would give him two fine golden babies with nothing but his love to help me.'

The young man looked at them in silence; then he said to the youngest: 'I think that you make the best offer. Will you be my wife?'

She smiled and said: 'I will that.'

'But see that you keep your promise or I'll turn you out.'

So it was agreed, and they went together to his father's fine house where they were married with great splendour. Then they settled down to enjoy their happiness.

The man gave his wife one of the household servants all to herself. This was a sharp-eyed, sharp-tongued young woman, quick and clever and well-thought-of. But she had no wish to remain a servant all her days, and at once she made up her mind to do the young wife harm.

One day the young wife told her husband that very soon she would keep her promise and bear him two golden babies. He was greatly pleased and made all preparations for them. But when the time came he was away from home, and the servant alone was there to take care of the wife.

Directly the babies were born the servant took them outside and threw them on the rubbish heap.

Then she ran to the stable where a bitch had just had a litter of puppies, took two of them, and put them into a basket.

Just then the husband returned home. The servant ran to him, crying: 'Look, master! See what fine sons your wife has borne you.'

He looked at the whimpering little beasts and at once fell into a rage, shouting at his wife and calling her terrible names. Then he turned her out of the house and made her live in the stables and do all the worst tasks of the household, while he took the servant in and made her his wife.

The golden babies soon died and their bodies were swallowed up by the rubbish heap. After a time the rubbish decayed and gardeners spread it on the ground. Two trees sprang out of the ground and grew quickly. Blossom came on them and then fruit, fine golden apples which shone in the sun, so that everyone for miles around came to marvel at the sight.

When she saw the trees the servant was filled with great dread. She thought for a while, and then said to the master who was now her husband: 'I sleep so badly these nights. It is time we had a new bed. Let us have those two trees cut down and made into a fine new bed. Then we shall lie at ease.'

He had no wish to do this, for, like everyone else, he had come to admire the trees for their great beauty. But still more he feared the lash of his new wife's tongue, and she kept at him day and night until he agreed.

So the trees were felled, and workmen cut the wood up and made a big bed. It was so comfortable that the man soon fell asleep, but the servant lay awake, pleased with what she had done. Then she heard one of the bedposts say: 'Brother, are you awake?'

The other post said: 'Yes, sister. I can't get to sleep for the weight of the servant lying at my side. And you?'

'I am very happy. Our father is on my side and he lies lightly.'

Well, you may guess that the servant got no more sleep that night. In the morning she said: 'It won't do, husband. It is a wretched bed, and I have never had a worse night. You must destroy it.'

'What's that? Destroy a new bed and a fine one too? I slept well enough.'

'I don't care. The bed must go and it will go. I'll have no more of it.'

And she used so many words on him that in the end, to keep her quiet, he ordered the bed to be broken up and used for firewood.

The servant herself saw to the burning. She shut all the windows and doors very carefully so that no scrap of wood should escape the fire, but two sparks shot up the chimney and came down outside. Where they fell two bushes of herbs sprang up, filling the air with their sweet smell.

A young lamb used to wander in the garden. It had been brought up by hand and was everyone's pet, so that it went just where it pleased. One day it decided to make a meal of the herbs. At once its fleece turned the colour of gold, and everyone who saw it marvelled at its beauty. But when the servant saw the golden lamb she was filled with terror, but she hid her feelings from her husband.

She said to him one morning: 'My love, I am going to have a baby very soon. You must take good care of me and satisfy every wish I may have. Just at this moment I have a great craving for lamb's liver. Have the pet lamb killed at once. No other will do.'

The man had no wish to see his lamb killed, but what could he do? His wife would give him no peace until she had her way. So the lamb was killed and taken to the kitchen. The servant herself cut out the heart and the liver and gave them to a kitchen-maid, saying: 'Here, take these and wash them well in the river. See that you bring back every smallest bit, or I'll have you whipped.'

The maid took the meat and washed it carefully. She was afraid of her mistress and, because her hands were shaking, two tiny scraps of the meat dropped into the water and were swept away on the current. She went to the kitchen and said nothing, and her mistress ate her supper greedily.

Next day there was another wonder. People going down to the river saw on the bank two children, a boy and a girl, and both more beautiful than the day, and each playing with a golden ball. All who saw them were filled with joy, but as for the servant, her feelings were of terror and hatred. The children played all day, and then the miller's old mother took them home to stay with her.

A few days later the master invited everyone to a feast, and the old woman came bringing the two beautiful children with her. They all enjoyed themselves, eating and drinking, and when all were satisfied the master said: 'Now, sit down, all of you. It is story-time, and each one of you must tell us a good tale.'

One by one the villagers told their stories, until it came to the turn of the two beautiful children.

The boy and the girl stood side by side, and the boy began:

'There were once three sisters. A young man came home from the wars and heard them laughing, and he asked them what the joke was.'

The girl took up the tale: 'The first sister said: "If that young man marries me I'll make him a beautiful home." And the second sister said: "If the young man marries me I'll feed his family." And the third sister said: "If the young man marries me, I'll give him two beautiful golden babies." So he married her.'

'Yes,' went on the boy. 'Then she was given a servant all to herself. But that one was a wicked woman, and when the wife had two beautiful golden babies the servant threw them on the rubbish-heap and showed the master two puppies instead.'

At this point the servant interrupted: 'Do we have to sit here listening to this nonsense?'

'Go on, children,' said the master. 'This is a good story.'

So the children went on with their tale, about

the bed and the herbs and the lamb, and how the lamb's meat had been washed into the river.

'And then,' said the boy, 'it was washed up on the bank, and where it touched there we came, my sister and I, and the miller's mother kindly took us home. So here we stand now, before our father. But where is our mother?'

All the listeners were filled with wonder at the tale, but not all of them believed that it could be true. So the boy said: 'See and believe.' And he and his sister threw off their clothes, and what a wonderful sight! Their bodies shone like gold.

Well, after that there were no doubters. The father jumped up and took his children in his arms, and the tears ran down his cheeks. Friends ran to the stables and brought out the mother, all dressed in rags, and she too kissed her children and wept for joy. As for the wicked servant, when all the excitement was over at last and the master remembered her, she was nowhere to be seen. A swift horse was missing from the stable, and that country knew her no more. Who cared? The master and his wife wanted nothing but to enjoy the happiness of life with their golden twins.

CANADA

# THE LAST DANCE

T HIS man was a mighty warrior, none greater in all the land between the oceans. The whole tribe looked up to him, and there was not a maiden who would not be proud to become his bride.

None loved him more fiercely than one maiden and she the most beautiful and the cleverest. But he would have none of her. For him the thrill of the hunt mattered more than anything. There was no room in his heart for love.

One day she told him frankly that she wanted him as her man. He turned her away with scornful words, and it did not take long for her love to turn into hate.

Soon after this the warriors went hunting far to the north, and at the farthest point their leader fell ill. What was wrong not the wisest of his fellows could say, but he was hot and cold and he raved with many wild words. His companions lost all hope that he would recover, and only one of them, the warrior's brother, had any idea what to do. This man, the oldest of the hunters, had studied magic, and he knew that someone wished his brother ill and was set on bringing about his death. So he went to the river and prayed to the spirit of the waters to help him.

Suddenly the water stirred and out came the head of a terrible creature. It was huge with bright eyes and great branching horns. 'Why do you disturb my rest?' said the monster.

'I want my brother well again. I want to know what has made him ill.'

'A maiden has put her death-wish upon him. He turned her away harshly and in this way she will have her revenge.'

The man asked how he could save his brother's life.

'Do you fear me?' asked the guardian of the waters.

'No,' said the man, and it was true, because his fear for his brother's safety had cast out all other fears.

44

'Very well,' said the monster. 'Take your knife and scrape the coating from my horns.'

The brother did as he was told, although the great beast was truly terrifying at this close range. Soon he had a handful of powdered horn.

'Take it,' said the monster. 'Mix one half in a cup of wine and give it to your brother. The other half is for the maiden.'

With this the brother was content. He hurried back to camp, and gave his sick brother the drink. Almost at once the young man began to recover, and in a day his strength had come back to him. So the hunt went on.

When they had killed enough caribou to last the tribe through the winter the hunters returned to the tribe. That night there was a great feast to welcome them. All the maidens joined in a dance, and the warrior's rejected lover was their leader. She leapt and span like a wild woman and everyone marvelled at her strength and her grace. But the brother watched her closely and never spoke nor smiled.

She grew weary at last and very hot. The brother went and fetched a cup, filling it with wine and dropping a little powder into it. When she passed him on her next round of the dancing ground he gave her the cup. She tossed the drink down and handed him the cup without a word.

Now her dance began to change. At first she had been the most agile of the young girls. Now her steps gradually grew heavier, and as they did her face and body changed. With every stage of the dance she became older. Her companions dropped out of the dance to watch, and everyone saw the years weighing upon her. The brightness faded from her eyes and the glow from her cheeks. Deep lines appeared like cracks across her face, her hands dropped limply at her sides, and her legs began to totter. She danced on just the same, as if she did not realize what was happening to her. At last the music faltered and she fell to the ground, a very old woman.

No one said anything. All—warriors, elders, women, children—went silently to their tents. In a little while there was nothing on the dancing ground but a heap of grey powder that stirred in the wind and then blew away.

IRELAND

# WHO IS THE SILLIEST?

P AT and Sally had been married these fifty
years and never, or not often, a cross word
between them. Poor they were but as happy
as they had any right to be. Wasn't Pat
surprised then to come home from the
fields one day to find old Sally in tears?

'What's the matter, woman?' he said.

'Why wouldn't I be crying, then?' she
said. 'All these years we've been wed, and
here we are with no little ones to keep us
company in our old age.'

'It's late in the day for that kind of talk,'

said Pat. 'Let us be grateful that we have our health and a little something in the kitchen for our supper, and have no more of this foolishness.'

He went out to his work in the morning, leaving Sally doing nothing worse than sniffing a little and dabbing at her eyes. But when he came home at night, what a noise! It sounded as if all the cats in Connemara were singing together. There sat Sally with two of her cronies, all a-weeping and a-howling, and never a smell of supper on the hearth.

'This is more than enough,' said Pat. 'Forget this nonsense about babies we haven't had and are not like to have at our time of life.'

'Ah, Pat!' said old Sally. 'It's not the baby we're crying about now. It's much worse than that.'

'What is it then?' said Pat.

'See that sack of meal that fell out of the loft this afternoon,' said Sally. 'Just look where it fell. That's the very spot where I was going to stand the cradle for our little baby.'

'Well, what of it?' said Pat shortly, because he was wanting his supper.

'Why, don't you see, man? If our baby had been lying there, doing no harm to nobody, and that great sack had fallen on him, why, the darling little precious would have been squashed flat as that pancake I was going to cook for your supper.'

And she and her friends set up such a bawling and a bellowing that Pat was near enough deafened.

When the noise had died down a little old Pat said: 'I've lived my life these seventy years, near

enough, and I've seen all the world hereabouts, but foolishness like this I never thought to see. Now I'm off, because it doesn't seem that, however long I wait, I am getting any supper tonight. I'll be off on my travels, and I'll not come back till I have found another—man, woman, child, or beast—sillier than you. Goodnight to you.' And he slammed the door behind him.

Well, he went along and he went along, and many a fine sight he saw, until he came upon a crowd of men, all in a long line and all hanging onto a mighty long snake—why, a hundred yards or more of it—and it wriggling and tossing.

'Good man!' shouted the leader. 'Come and help hold this monster.'

'Where are you taking it?' said Pat.

'To the sea. It's a score of miles and more, but we've got no choice. This creature has been preying on us for years, but we've caught it at last. Now we are going to carry it to the sea and when we get there, why, we'll drop it in and drown it, the devil.'

'I'll give you a hand,' said Pat. 'Just put it down a minute and lend me that axe.'

They did as they were told, though it was clear they didn't like the idea. Pat picked up the axe, swung it over his head, and—clop!—cut the snake's head off very neatly.

'There you are,' he said. 'Now you needn't carry it so far.'

'Glory be!' said the men. 'It's nothing but a wonder you are. How ever did you think of that?'

Pat went on his way with no more words. Next

day, with the sun shining brightly, he came to a meadow where the hay lay half cut. The workers were sprawled in a heap in the middle of the field.

'You'd best get that hay finished soon. There's rain on the way,' said Pat.

'Blessings on you,' said the men. 'We have been waiting for such as you to come to our rescue. See, we ate our dinner an hour since, but somehow our legs all got tangled together as we lay here and now we can't get them sorted out. Can you help us, please?'

'Certainly,' said Pat. He picked up a bucket, filled it at the stream, and threw the lot over them. They all jumped up, yelling and gasping, and seemed to have no more trouble with knotted legs.

After a time Pat came to another field. The grain was just right for harvesting but the men were doing no work. They just stood in line, and, one by one, they took it in turns to walk along the line, counting.

'And what might you be up to?' said Pat.

'We're in a muddle,' said one of the men. 'Master sent us out to gather the harvest. There were thirteen of us when he counted us, but now we keep counting and it keeps coming to twelve. We can't start work until we are all here. Can you get us sorted out, mister?'

'Count them again,' said Pat. So the man went along the line, muttering 'One, two, three . . .' and at the end of the line 'twelve'.

'There you are,' he said. 'Still one missing.'

'You didn't count yourself,' said Pat.

'Course I didn't,' said the man. 'Master didn't count himself neither, and he made it thirteen.'

'Line up again,' said Pat, 'and I'll count you.' And he did, and it came to thirteen.

'That's wonderful,' said all the men. 'But where did you find the thirteenth man, mister?'

'In the madhouse,' said Pat rudely.

'Surely I've seen enough sillies,' he said to himself, and headed for home.

He had not gone far when he came up with an old, old woman, all dressed in coloured rags with a ribbon in her hair and singing fit to burst.

'Good day to you, mister,' she said. 'Have you seen the King?'

'Have I seen the what?' said Pat.

'The High King himself,' said the old crone. 'They say he's travelling the length of the country looking for a wife, and why wouldn't he be choosing me? They say I'm the fairest beauty in all this land.'

'Who said that, and when?'

'An old travelling tinker told me, it must be thirty, forty years past.'

'Well, I'll tell you a secret,' said Pat. 'I'm the High King myself.'

'You don't look like him,' said the old woman.

'Ah, that's because I'm travelling in disguise. Now I don't fancy that I'll find a finer woman than yourself today or any day and, what's more, I guess that you cook a good dinner when you've a mind to it.'

'That I can,' said the woman. 'Just you come

home with me now, and I'll cook you a meal you won't forget in a lifetime.'

So she took Pat home and he ate until he could scarcely stir a limb.

'Now,' said she. 'Let us go find the priest and he will marry us.'

'Not such a hurry,' said Pat. 'It wouldn't do at all for the High King to be married in these clothes. I'll just get along to my palace and put on my crown and robes.'

He hurried away at his best speed. He had not gone far when he came upon a man and a boy. They had their arms round a donkey and were trying to lift him.

'What would you be doing?' asked Pat.

'It's this donkey,' gasped the man. 'You see that long grass growing among the thatch on our roof? Every year we make him eat it, and every year he gets heavier to lift onto the roof.'

'Is there no other way?' said Pat.

'Hardly. We can't take the roof off and put it on the ground for him, can we?'

'Let me try it my way,' said Pat, and he took a scythe and with a quick scritch-scritch he cut all the grass. He tossed it to the ground and the donkey ate it with no trouble at all.

'You're the world's wonder,' said the man.

'And you're the world's booby,' said Pat, and he went home.

There sat Sally, so glad to see him that she quite forgot to cry about her baby and the sack.

'Well, Sally my dear,' said Pat. 'I've travelled

the world now, and I've seen sillies who make you just about the wisest woman in the world. Am I not the lucky one to have you to wonder at for the rest of my days?'

And why shouldn't they be living happily for ever after?

GERMANY

# MASTER OF HIS TRADE

HANS and Trudi were poor. They were sitting outside their hut one evening, resting after the day's toil, when a fine carriage stopped. A fine gentleman got down and said: 'Greetings, old folks. I have taken a fancy to eat a simple country meal. Will you let me sit at your table and share your food?'

For sure they had little enough for themselves, but Hans bowed and said: 'You are welcome, sir.' Then they went in and ate, and poor food it was too and little of it.

Afterwards they sat while the stranger smoked his pipe.

Hans said: 'I have still a little work to do. Will you walk into the garden while I finish my task?' There was a young tree waiting to be planted, and the old man set about digging a hole and driving in a post. 'That is heavy work,' said the stranger. 'Have you no son to help you?' 'No,' said old Hans. 'I had a son once but he was no good. He was too clever to work, and he went out into the world and came to a bad end, I expect.'

By this time Hans had planted his tree and tied it well. Nearby a twisted tree was growing. 'Why don't you tie that one the same way and get it to grow straight?' said the stranger.

Hans smiled. 'It's too late,' he said. 'I should have tied it when it was young and easily trained. It will never be any good now.'

'That was the trouble with your son,' said the stranger. 'If you had trained him better he would have done well. Now he too is twisted into the wrong shape.'

'It's so long since I saw him,' said Hans sadly. 'I wouldn't know him now.'

'Had he no marks by which you would know him?'

'Why, yes,' said the old man. 'He had a star on his left shoulder.'

'Like this?' said the stranger, and he slipped down the sleeve of his shirt, and there was a mark like a star.

'Yes,' said old Hans. 'You are my son,' and he

threw his arms around him. 'But you have done well in the world. You dress like a lord, and talk like one too.'

'I have grown up twisted,' said the son. 'I am a thief. Don't be alarmed. I'm not your common thief but a master of my trade. There is none better in the kingdom. You may yet be proud of me.'

'But a thief!' said the old man. 'I can't and I won't be pleased about that. But you are still my son and I love you.' And he took him indoors and told Trudi, who wept a little and held her son close to her heart.

'Do you remember the lord of the castle who stood sponsor for you when you were baptized? He is still alive. He is a just man but a strong man too. If he hears that you are a thief he won't be slow in hanging you on the end of a rope. Best keep away from the castle.'

'Don't worry, father. I intend to visit him tomorrow.'

And in the morning the thief went to the castle where, because he was dressed well and drove up in a fine carriage, he was brought at once to the lord.

'Good morning, my lord. You will not remember me, but I am old Hans' son and your own godson. Now I have been out in the world and become a master thief.'

'Your own words condemn you,' said the lord. 'But you are still my godson. I held you in my arms at the font, and I will not willingly give you to the hangman. Prove your words; I will set you three tasks. You must steal my horse. You must steal my wife's wedding ring from her finger and the sheet from our bed. You must steal the parson and his clerk from out of his church. If you fail I will not stand between you and the law, and the law says that you must die.'

'Very well,' said the thief. 'It shall be done.' And he bowed low and bade the lord farewell.

Now watch closely and you will see how a master thief goes to work.

He puts on the ragged clothes of an old peasant woman. He rubs stain on his face and arms and paints wrinkles on his face so that his own mother wouldn't know him. He gets a wine cask and fills it with a mixture of good wine and strong sleeping herbs. He takes the cask on his back and totters up to the castle.

It is getting dark. He sits down, and starts coughing and banging himself with his arms as if he is cold. One of the guards sitting by a fire calls out: 'Come over here, mother. Have a warm.' He goes to the fire, and the soldier helps him off with the cask. 'My word, that's heavy,' he says. 'What have you got in it?' 'The best wine,' he says. 'That's my trade, buying and selling. Try a drop.' So the soldier helps himself, and then he has another, and he calls his friends over and they all drink deep. They begin to sing and shout as the wine grips them, and their fellows guarding the stable call out: 'What's going on?'

'Good wine, that's what's going on, and going down too. Come and get your share.'

'Send her in here. We can't leave the horses.'

So the thief takes the wine to the stable. There are three guards. One is sitting astride the horse, one holds the bridle, and the third is hanging onto the horse's tail. They are all very thirsty and they drink eagerly of the old woman's wine. Before long they are asleep, two lying on the floor, the third still in the saddle. The thief takes four ropes, two hanging from each of the opposite walls of the stable, and he ties them to the corners of the saddle so that it holds steady. Then he carefully walks the horse forward, leaving the soldier still sitting on

the saddle in mid-air. Lastly he jumps on the horse and gallops away, leaving all the soldiers in their drunken sleep.

Next morning the thief rides the horse back to the castle. The lord has just got up and is looking out of the window. 'Good morning, my lord,' says the thief. 'Here is your horse. I stole him from the stable last night. You will find his guards lying around but they won't remember what happened.'

'So much for the first task,' says the lord. 'The second will not be so easy.'

That night the lord said to his wife: 'The thief will come tonight, but I'll be ready for him. I'll sit up and as soon as he shows himself I'll blow his head off.' So there he sat, holding his gun, while his lady lay in bed clutching her wedding ring.

The thief went into the town. The lord had been handing out justice during the day, and one poor rogue still hung on the gallows. The thief cut him down and carried the body up to the castle. He put a ladder under the bedroom window and began to climb up, holding the dead man on his shoulders. As soon as the head appeared at the window the lord fired and the thief let the body drop to the ground.

'I got him first shot,' said the lord to his wife. 'I'd better bury him rightaway and then no one need ever know.' And he went downstairs. When the lord had picked up the body and taken it away to the garden, the thief ran up the ladder and climbed into the bedroom. 'Well, he's dead all right,' he said to the lady. 'He was a villain, but after all he was my godson and I'll not shame him. Here, let me have the sheet to wrap him in. I won't let him lie like a dog.' He took the sheet off the bed, then said: 'No one could call me an unjust man. The poor devil risked his life to get your wedding ring. He shall have it. I'll bury it with him.' The lady was not too pleased about this, but she pulled off her ring, and the thief took it and the sheet away.

The lord was sleepy and ill-tempered after his restless night when the thief arrived, full of high spirits, and handed him his sheet and ring. 'How did you get out of your grave?' said the lord.

'Did your master, the devil himself, help you?'

'Fair's fair,' said the thief. 'You hanged a rogue yesterday. It was only right that you should have the job of burying him.'

'Two points to you,' said the lord with a sour smile. 'But it is the third that counts. The rope is still waiting for you.'

At night the thief made his way to the church-yard, carrying a lantern. On his back he had a big sack which, if you could have seen it in the dark, seemed to wriggle and heave. In the churchyard he took out a bundle of candles and lit them. Then he opened the sack and out came a lot of live crabs. He stuck a lighted candle on the back of each crab, and they scuttled around the churchyard carrying their lights with them. The thief draped himself from head to foot in a long black robe, like a preacher, picked up the sack, and went into church. He climbed up into the pulpit and began to shout: 'Hear ye! The end is at hand. Sinners, repent before it is too late. See, the dead have come out of their graves and are seeking their bones, each carrying its own light. Come and be saved while yet there is time.'

He made a terrible noise. It could be heard right in the village, but the parson and his clerk, who lived just outside the church, heard it first, and it gave them a rare fright. They crept into church. The thief saw them and bellowed, louder than ever: 'Sinners, come to repentance. I am Peter who holds the keys of heaven. Climb into this sack and I will take you there. Hurry now or it will be too late.'

The clerk said to the parson: 'That seems a fair offer. Shall we take advantage of it, your reverence?'

'We had better,' said the parson, and the two climbed into the sack and the thief drew the opening tight. They were a good weight and he found he could not lift them, so he dragged the sack behind him. They bumped down the pulpit steps, and he shouted: 'We are going over the mountains.' Outside, it had started to rain, and there were big puddles everywhere. He pulled the sack through them and said: 'The clouds are wet tonight.' He reached the castle steps, crying: 'Now we ascend to the gates of heaven.' He heaved the sack into the dovecote and all the pigeons went up in a wild flutter of wings. 'Hark!' he cried. 'The angels are welcoming you.' Then he locked them in and went home to bed.

In the morning he stood before the lord in the great hall. 'Where are the parson and his clerk?' said the lord. 'It seems that you have failed.'

'Send to the dovecote and you will find them,' said the thief. 'Treat them gently. They think they are in heaven.'

The lord wanted to see for himself, so he went to the dovecote and let the two ninnies free. He was hard put to it not to laugh, but he kept a straight face and a harsh voice and said to the thief: 'You have proved yourself. You are the master of all thieves. But thieves I will not have in my land. Go, and if I find you here again you hang without fail.'

So the thief said goodbye to his old mother and father and went out into the wide world, where, I do not doubt, he prospered greatly.

ITALY

# ANSWER THE RIDDLE

THE king was out hunting the deer. He became thirsty and stopped at a cottage to ask for a drink. Then, as he liked to know how his subjects lived, he said to the peasant who had served him: 'How much do you earn?'

'Fourpence a day, Sire.'

'That's a lot of money. And how do you spend it?'

The peasant said: 'I eat one penny. I invest one. I give one back, and the last penny I throw away.'

The king smiled and rode on. Then it struck him that the peasant's reply had been a strange one, so he turned his horse and went back.

'Tell me,' he said. 'What did you mean—you eat one penny, invest one, give one back, and throw one away?'

The peasant said: 'It's simple. First I must feed myself. Then I feed my children who will take care of me when I am old. Then I feed my father and pay him back for all he has done for me. Lastly I feed the wife, and that does me no good at all.'

'Very good!' said the king and he laughed heartily. 'Now listen,' and he gave him a coin. 'Don't tell anyone else what you have just told me. It will be our secret for ever, or at least until you have looked on my face a hundred times.'

That evening, when he had dined and was sitting at his ease with his councillors, the king began to chuckle. He said: 'Here is a riddle. A man earns fourpence a day. He eats one penny, he invests one, he gives one back, and he throws one away. How do you explain that?'

The wisest men in the kingdom were sitting there, but not one of them could come up with the right answer.

'If you can't find the answer you are not fit to be my advisers,' said the king.

One of the councillors remembered that he had seen the king that day talking to a peasant. As soon as he could get away he rode back to the village and found the man.

'I'm sorry,' said the peasant. 'I'd like to tell you

the answer, but I promised the king I would tell no one, at least not until I had looked on his face a hundred times.'

'Oh,' said the councillor, 'I think I can help you there.'

He felt in his purse and pulled out a handful of coins. 'Here,' he said, 'are a hundred pennies. Look at them closely. The king's face is stamped on each one.'

The peasant studied each coin before putting it safely into his bag. Then he said: 'Now I have looked at the king's royal face a hundred times. The answer is ...,' and he told the councillor the whole riddle.

At dinner that night the councillor said: 'Sire, I have the answer to your riddle,' and he told him, and he was right in every word. The king was not pleased. He nodded sourly, and next morning he sent for the peasant.

'Now, you rogue,' he said, 'did I not tell you to keep your riddle to yourself until you had seen me a hundred times?'

'Sire,' said the peasant, 'with the help of your wise councillor I have had the honour of gazing on Your Majesty's lovely face just so many times. See,' and he opened his bag and showed the king the pile of coins.

The king was much amused that it had cost his councillor so dearly to gain wisdom. He made up his mind to keep that clever man firmly in his place in future, but the peasant he rewarded with a generous gift of gold.

69

TURKEY

# THE PRINCE WHO WOULD
# BE YOUNG FOR EVER

WHEN the prince was born it seemed that he must be the happiest child on earth, for the king and queen, his parents, were rich and powerful, and they loved him beyond everything.

Yet he was an unhappy baby. Day and night he screamed, and nothing that anyone might do would content him. The king promised him all the kingdoms of the world; he screamed. He should have for his wife the most beautiful princess between the oceans; he screamed. At last the king

said: 'Only be quiet, and I will give you eternal youth.' The baby fell silent and lay contentedly in his cot.

As the baby grew into a boy, and the boy into a young man, he was given everything that the king's wealth and power and influence could command. Above all he studied with the wisest men in the kingdom and grew daily in knowledge and wisdom, so that all the people wondered to see so wise and understanding a young man.

He was fifteen. There was a feast to celebrate his birthday, and all was jollity. Then the prince stood up and said: 'Father, give me what you promised me as a baby.'

'Come, come, my son,' said the king. 'That was nothing but a joke made to keep you quiet. I give you everything I have, but what I don't possess you must do without.'

The prince said: 'If you cannot give me eternal youth I will go and find it for myself.'

The queen fell on her knees beside him. 'Don't leave us, son,' she said. 'The king is old and tired now, and you must stay to rule the kingdom in his place. Stay, and we will find the loveliest princess to be your bride.'

But the prince would not change his mind. Into the world he must go to find the eternal youth that was his birthright.

He made ready for his journey. His father's stables were full of fine horses. He picked out the strongest and tallest stallion, and laid his hand on its side. At once the great horse began to quiver and shake and all the strength ran out of it. The same happened in turn to all the other horses; not one of them could bear his touch.

He looked around in despair. In a dark corner of the stable was tied a poor old horse, scarcely more than a bag of bones held together with skin; its eyes were clouded and its back was one big open sore. He went over and put one hand gently upon its flank. The horse lifted its head and said: 'What do you want of me, my lord? Thanks be that at last a great warrior needs my help.'

Then a great shudder ran through it. It stood up straight and firm on its thin legs.

'What must I do?' asked the prince humbly.

'First you must build me up,' said the horse. 'I have been sorely neglected. Give me good food and groom me daily for six weeks. This you must do yourself, for the poor creatures who look after your stables will not heal me. Then, when I am strong, bid the king give you the weapons and armour that he had as a young man. None other will do.'

So that is what the prince did. He searched the armoury until he found his father's ancient weapons, and very rusty they were too. He worked on them with his own hands, sharpening and polishing until they shone and their blades would cut a single hair floating in the wind. As for the old horse, he fed him until the bones were hidden by good solid flesh, and combed and brushed him until the coat shone fine and silky.

Now it was time to go. The prince looked very fine in his shining armour and mounted on his horse. The king had insisted that he take with him an army of a thousand men, all armed, as well as a train of mules laden with treasure and rich food. So the prince rode out, and all the people cheered and the women wept.

When he reached the borders of his father's kingdom, the prince sent all the soldiers back, and he made them take their mules with them. Then he went on alone, with only his horse for company.

After days of travel they came to a land where the earth was stricken and bare and the bones of many men littered the ground. The prince wondered much at this, and the horse said: 'Here lives a wicked witch. She hates all men and kills any who come into her country. Take care that your weapons are ready, for you will need them soon.' So they travelled on until night came, and then they took it in turns to sleep and keep watch.

In the morning, just as the prince was mounted, there was a terrible noise and a great wind shook the trees. 'The witch is coming,' said the horse, and she rushed towards them. The prince lashed out with his sword and cut off one of her feet. She screamed hoarsely, and he raised his hand to strike again.

'No more, young prince,' she shouted. 'Let us make peace.' And the prince was content to do so.

'Take care of that horse,' said the witch. 'It has more magic in its hind hoof than I have in my whole body. Why, if you had not been riding it I would have had your life today and would have eaten you for supper. As it is, we will sit down together and feast, and that is something that no other human has ever done.'

They feasted well, but suddenly the witch began to groan and scream. 'My foot hurts,' she cried. The prince tossed her the foot he had cut off, and she fitted it back neatly into its place and felt much better. They became merry together, and the witch begged the prince to stay with her and marry the prettiest of her daughters. The prince would have none of this, and after some days of joyful living he rode away on his adventure.

In time the road led through a country where all the trees and plants had been burnt to ashes. The horse said: 'Now we are in the land of another witch, sister of her we just met and far more horrible. See that your sword is loose in its sheath.'

Next morning there was a fearful noise and the smell of smoke. Then a cloud of smoke and flame came towards them, and in the heart of it a gigantic witch with three hideous heads. The prince drew his sword and gave one hearty blow, which took off the ugliest of the heads. At once the witch pleaded for mercy, and the prince went cheerfully with her to her house. There they feasted, and the prince gave her back her head, which she set in its place and no harm done. She would have liked him to stay there for ever, but the prince would not be kept from his quest.

So in time they went on their way. Now they found themselves in a country where the air was soft and sweet-scented and flowers grew everywhere.

The horse said: 'We are come into the land of eternal youth. It is always spring here. The castle of youth is just a day's journey away, but it is guarded by terrible monsters. They are so many that not even your good sword could cut off all their heads. We must avoid them. We will rest today, and in the morning we shall be fresher for the contest.'

They stood on a high hill looking over the forest to the towers of the castle. 'All the monsters are feeding in the forest,' said the horse. 'With good luck we may miss them. Tighten my girths and hold on very fast, for now we must jump.'

Up into the air they went and over the trees. Below lay the castle, all glowing in the sun. Now they began to drop, and the horse's hind hoofs just touched the topmost twig of a tree. At once there was a howl as all the monsters sprang up, ready to defend the castle.

The prince and his horse landed in the court-yard. A hundred monsters were within reach and would surely have torn man and horse to shreds, but the lady of the castle was at hand. She loved to feed her kittens (as she called the dreadful beasts) with her own hands. At sight of the handsome young man and his fine steed she called back her guardians and ordered them to go into the forest. Then she held out her hands and bade the prince welcome.

'My castle is yours,' she said. 'How can I help you?'

'I am looking for eternal youth,' said the prince.

'You need look no more,' she said. 'It is here.' So

they went in and feasted most royally. The horse was not forgotten, for he had the finest golden hay, all that he could eat and more. So the days passed, quickly and happily.

'Why not stay here for ever?' said the lady of the castle one day.

'I will most surely, if I may live here with you as my wife.'

So it was, and they lived together in great contentment. The lady gave the prince the freedom of her land where he might go as he wished. 'Only one valley you must not enter, or it will bring you sorrow,' she said.

Hunting was one of the prince's greatest pleasures. The land was full of game, and he enjoyed many a day's good sport, riding from morning to sunset. One day he started a hare and rode after it in great excitement. He shot an arrow but missed, and did the same with the next. The failure annoyed him, for he rarely missed his mark, so he rode on, not thinking where the chase was taking him. Without realizing it he had ridden into the forbidden valley. All at once darkness came into his heart. For the first time since he set out on his quest he thought of his father and mother, and he was seized with a deep longing to see them again. Tears came into his eyes, and he could not hide his unhappiness.

'You have been in the forbidden valley,' said the lady when she saw him.

'I am sorry,' he said. 'I did not wish to go there, but now I cannot rest until I see my people again.

Let me return home, and I will come back quickly and never again part from you.'

'It will do you no good,' said the lady, but no words of hers could make him forget his longing for home. Home he must go, whatever the cost.

'You are a fool,' said the horse. 'But you have been a good master to me and I will take you home. But remember this; if you get off my back I shall return without you.'

'I will remember,' said the prince. He said farewell to his lady, and she wept bitterly and would not be comforted. Then he rode away.

The prince and his horse passed through the lands of the two witches, but they looked quite different. The scorched ground and the forests had all gone. Rich cornfields shone golden in the sun, and there were many fine houses and cities. The prince spoke to some of the people he saw about the witches, but they all laughed at him. 'Fairy tales!' they said. 'Yes, we have heard about the terrible sisters, but it was all so long ago and no one believes in them any more.'

'How can that be?' said the prince. 'Why, I was with them only a few weeks ago.' But they only laughed the more, and little boys threw stones at him.

He rode on. He felt very weary and the way seemed long, but he never noticed that his hair was turning white. Nothing he saw as he passed was as he remembered it, and this made him angry. His hands shook and his grip on the horse's flanks became weak. A white beard flowed down over his chest almost to his waist, but still he did not notice anything strange.

So he came home. The city he knew so well had changed greatly with many new buildings, bigger and richer than any he remembered. The palace still stood in its old place but he scarcely recognized it. In the courtyard he swung his leg over the horse and began to dismount.

'Take care, master,' said the horse. 'Once you are on the ground I must go back. Stay mounted and we will return to where you belong.'

'No, I must go on,' said the prince. 'Thank you for your help, old friend. I will follow after you as quickly as I can.'

He climbed to the ground and at once the horse ran off, swift as an arrow.

The palace stood deserted. It was half in ruin and weeds grew in the throne room. Even the chapel looked neglected with a crumbling roof. He went inside and saw, showing all the signs of great age, the ancient tombs of his father and mother. Nearby a coffin lay on the ground. A golden plate was let into the lid, and on this he read his own name. He pulled up the lid with a great effort. It was empty. The hinges squeaked, and a very old and rusty voice seemed to say: 'Welcome. You have kept us waiting.' And the prince fell forward into the coffin and crumbled into dust.

PORTUGAL

# A CAT'S TALE

A HANDSOME cat-about-town went to the barber's to have his whiskers trimmed.

'And will there be anything else, sir?' said the barber. 'What about your tail? It could perhaps do with just a couple of inches off the tip.'

'Very well,' said the cat, 'but be careful not to take too much. My tail is much admired.'

So the barber clipped the end of the tail, thinking: 'This will make a fine shaving brush.' The cat set off for home, twirling his whiskers and swinging what was left of his tail. Suddenly he stopped and said to himself: 'Whatever am I thinking of? That barber has got my tail for nothing.' And he returned to the barber's shop and demanded to have it back.

'Sorry, sir. It can't be done.'

'Then I'll take one of your razors.'

On his way Puss passed through the market where he saw an old fishwife trying to cut up a fish with a blunt knife. 'Here, my good woman,' he said. 'Accept this razor with my good wishes.' Then he continued on his journey, well pleased with his own kindness.

It was not long before he had second thoughts.

> *'That's a fine razor*
> *Good as new*
> *It must be worth*
> *A pound or two.*

I'll have it back'.

But do you think the old woman would give up the razor? Not she. So Puss took one of her herrings instead.

It was dinner time, and the cat noticed a poor old miller sitting by the roadside wearing away what was left of his teeth on a hunk of dry bread. 'You can do better than that, my man,' said the cat. 'Now take this excellent herring, and welcome to it.'

Soon he was regretting his generosity.

*'Surely that fish*
*Would make a dish*
*Both rich and fat*
*Fit for this cat.*

I'll get it back.'

The herring was safely inside the miller, so Puss took one of his bags of flour.

Puss's journey took him past the village school. He heard a great noise of crying and wailing, and looking inside he found all the children making a fuss because they were hungry. 'Dear children,' he said, 'take this bag of flour. Your teacher will make you a nice cake with it.'

'How good it is to make people happy!' thought Puss as he walked on. Then he stopped and said: 'But what about my happiness? Wouldn't I enjoy that cake?' He hurried back to the school, but the flour was already gone.

'Right,' said the cat. 'I'll have one of your girls instead.' And he picked a sturdy little girl and dragged her away.

Next he came to the laundry. The poor laundress was working hard, struggling to do all the washing and ironing without any help. 'This will never do,' said the cat. 'Take this little girl. You will find her a grand worker.'

What do you think? In no time at all the cat was sorry for what he had done. He went back to the laundry, but the laundress would not give up her new helper. 'Very well,' said the cat, and he took one of the newly ironed shirts.

On he went until he came upon a street musician playing his fiddle and getting very few pennies for his pains. Oh, he was a poor fellow with not a shirt to his back. 'You'll never get anywhere looking like that,' said Puss. 'Smarten yourself up and you will find that the money will come rolling in. Here, take this shirt and put it on at once.'

But while the man was putting on his shirt the cat stole his fiddle. He ran up a tree out of reach, and sat there scraping a tune and singing:

> 'I lost my tail and won a razor,
> Lost the razor, found a fish.
> Fish went missing, got some flour,
> Swapped the flour for a lass.
> Lassie left, so took a shirt.
> Shirt produced this noble fiddle,
> So here I sing "Hey-diddle-diddle".'

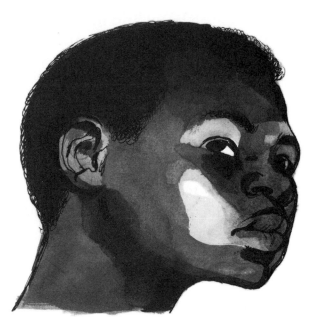

NIGERIA

# ONCE POOR, POOR FOR EVER

IN THE village there were two men, one poor, the other rich. The first, oh, he was just as miserable as you could imagine. He never had any money, and the very food he ate was other people's leavings. As for the rich man, he had everything: wife and children, servants, a fine house, fruitful land. What made it worse was that the two men lived side by side, so no one could fail to see the difference between them.

One day a beggar came to the village. At least he looked like a beggar, ragged clothes and begging bowl and all, but in fact he was the richest man in the country. It amused him to walk among the people, unknown, and to see how he might help those who deserved it.

He saw the rich man standing outside his grand house. 'Blessings on you and yours,' he said.

'Be off with you, you rogue,' said the rich man. 'You'll get nothing here. We don't allow beggars in this village. All they can expect is a sound beating.'

So the very rich beggar went on and came to the wretched hut and miserable fields belonging to the poor man. The poor man was toiling away, scraping the soil and trying his best to coax some maize to grow. 'Blessings on you and your work,' said the beggar.

'Blessings on you too, your honour,' said the poor man. He got up and shouted: 'Wife, we have a guest. Bring him food and drink.' So she did, but all she could offer were a few dried beans and a cup of dirty water. 'We can only give you what we eat ourselves,' she said.

He took the food and said: 'Thanks to God for these blessings, and thanks too to you good people.' He touched the food and drink lightly with his lips, but ate nothing.

Then he went home to his fine palace in the city and thought to himself: 'That poor wretch was prepared to give me everything he had. I must reward him.' He thought for a while. Then he sent for a big bowl which he filled almost to the brim with silver coins. He covered it with a grass mat to hide what was inside. Then he called his little

daughter and they went back to the village together, she carrying the bowl.

All the people were working in the fields, even the rich man. 'See that poor man over there,' he said to his daughter. 'Tell him this is a gift.' So she went and offered the bowl to the poor man. He guessed that it must be full of food. Not daring to lift the mat because he was sure that, seeing the food, he would not be able to resist gobbling it all up, he said to the girl: 'Take it first to my good neighbour over there. Ask him to take what he wants and let me have what is left.'

She took the bowl to the rich man. He looked inside and saw the money. He quickly filled his pockets, and then put a handful or two of flour into the bowl. 'Here, girl,' he said. 'Take it back to my neighbour. Tell him I have had enough. He is welcome to what is left.'

When the poor man saw that there was flour in the bowl he was very happy. 'Glory be to God,' he said to his wife. 'We shall eat well tonight, thanks to this fine gift.'

The very rich man saw what had happened. He said to his daughter: 'If you were to lay a block of gold in that fool's path he would only trip over it and break his stupid neck. I wanted to change his fortune, but he is determined to hold onto the bad luck he was born with. Who am I to interfere?'

And he went back to his rich palace.

# A WOMAN WHO HAD
# THE SIGHT

THE old midwife of Garth Dorwen had plied
her trade for many a year; in fact half the
folk of Caernarfon had been brought into
the world with her help. Now, feeling it
was time she took life more easily, she went
into town to the hiring fair to find herself a
servant.

She noticed a pretty young girl with a
mop of fair hair standing apart in the
marketplace. She spoke to her and liked
her manners and what she had to say for
herself, so she struck a bargain with her
right away. This girl's name was Eilian.

A good worker she turned out to be, quick and clean, and always ready with a willing hand and a cheerful word. Only one habit bothered the old nurse; when the moon was full Eilian liked to take her spinning-wheel outside and work all evening at the river's edge. The amount of work she got through during these evenings was remarkable, and the old woman wondered at it and at the sounds of music and laughter that came up from the meadow. Eilian never said a word when she came home, and the nurse had to be satisfied that her servant was so capable a worker and so happy.

The winter went by. One spring morning Eilian did not come to breakfast, and the mistress could find no trace of her in her room. Nor did Eilian return, although the old woman looked for her everywhere.

So spring and summer passed. On a dark night in early winter, when drizzling rain hid the full moon, a strange gentleman rode up to the door. His wife was in labour, and the old woman's skills were needed urgently. She was used to such calls, so she climbed up behind him without any fuss, and they rode through the dark night to a house in a part of the country where she had never been. She followed the man through a grand hall into a bedroom where a fine lady lay in pain. She set to work and before the night was out a healthy baby had been born.

The old nurse was kept so busy that it was some time before she noticed a strange thing; although the house was furnished with everything one might wish for and good food was always on the table, there were no servants, and she never saw anyone but the husband and wife and the little baby. Well, that was odd, but after all it was none of her business, and she had enough to keep herself occupied without pushing her nose in where it did not belong.

One morning the gentleman brought her a jar of ointment. 'This is for the baby's eyes,' he said. 'Just a small dab will be enough to treat each eye. Be very careful, and whatever you do keep it away from your own eyes or you will be sorry.'

She did as she was told, and the baby seemed no better and no worse for it. But afterwards her own left eye began to itch, and without thinking she rubbed it with the finger that had touched the ointment.

Now, what a wonderful change! Her right eye still saw the same fine rooms with their rich hangings and splendid furniture. The left eye showed her a damp and dreary cave. In one corner, lying on a heap of rushes she saw her servant Eilian. Little men and women went and came all the time, waiting on Eilian, bringing her food, and caring for her most tenderly.

Towards evening the old nurse said: 'What a lot of people have been in and out today, Eilian.'

'So they have, to be sure,' said the girl, 'but how did you know me?'

The nurse confessed that she had accidentally rubbed her eye with the ointment.

'Don't let my husband find out,' said Eilian.
Then she told her story, how the small folk had
helped her with her spinning and had pestered her
to marry their chief. She resisted them for several
weeks, threatening them with her knife (for they
were greatly afraid of iron) and keeping a branch of
rowan wood beside her bed at night. Then, after a
busy day, she had become careless and forgot to
renew the rowan branch. They came for her that
night, and she had lived with them ever since. She
had borne them a future chief, and now she was
tied to them for ever.

After a few more days Eilian and the baby were
strong enough to be left, and the husband took the

old nurse home. He paid her well and she thanked
him, but she gave no hint that she could see him as
he really was.

A week or two later the old woman went to
market. When she got there one of her gossips said
to her: 'What a terrible day! The prices have gone
mad and they are just going up and up. For sure the
fairies must be here.'

The old woman looked round her. Her right eye
saw only the familiar sights of the market. With her
left she saw that there were little people everywhere, mixing up the price tickets, upsetting the
stalls and muddling all the goods, stealing whatever took their fancy. Foremost among them was

Eilian's husband. She watched him at his mischief and then followed him to the tavern where he stopped for a drink.

'Good morning, master,' she said. 'It's a fine day for the fair, and a fine day for bargains to be had by those who don't bother to pay.'

'Good morning, mistress,' he replied. 'And what is that supposed to mean?'

'Take it as you will,' she said. 'And how is my servant Eilian?'

He stared at her closely. 'She is well,' he said, 'but tell me, mistress, with which eye do you see me now?'

'With the left.'

Without another word he threw his ale into her face. It burned like fire and her eyes flowed with tears from the pain. When they stopped running he had vanished, and never again did she see any of the little folk or her young servant Eilian.

ETHIOPIA

# SLAYER OF THOUSANDS

A FINE prince he was! No one in the kingdom was more handsome, and he was quick-witted with it. As for talking, he would spin words like a spider spins thread.

Just one thing spoiled his father's pride in him; the prince had about as much courage as an old ewe.

Well, we can't all be brave. But the king, expecting that his son would be as bold as a lion—or as his father—had given him the name Shi-Guday, which means Slayer of

Thousands! When he thought about the name and all his hopes and then saw how his son had turned out, the king felt such a fool.

Every year there was a great hunt, and every year the prince managed to get himself left behind when the warriors marched off to the hunting grounds. But a year came when the king was determined that his son must be put to the test. Whatever excuses the young man made were useless; a-hunting he must go.

Off they went, each warrior eager to be the first to make contact with a lion. Each one? Well, there was Shi-Guday! He managed to take the wrong track quite early in the chase and he soon lost all sight and sound of the hunting party. Very soon he was quite lost. At first it was good to be free from the perils of the chase. Then it came to him that no one was at hand to protect him from the wild beasts of the forest. When this dawned on him he started running, and the greater his fear grew the farther he ran away from the hunters.

The light began to fade. Night was coming with its greater perils. Shi-Guday thought he would be safer up a tree, so he climbed as high as he dared, shaking with fear as the night filled with the hunting cries of wild animals. There was one scream louder and more terrifying than all the rest. It was enough to freeze the blood. The prince gave a start and fell out of the tree.

He landed on something surprisingly soft. He was sitting astride some animal. It must be big, but it was too dark to see just what it was. The beast ran off with Shi-Guday clinging tight to its shaggy coat. It gave out one ear-piercing scream after another, and so did Shi-Guday. 'Ooer ooer!' he cried, and each yell seemed to make his mount go faster. So the prince rode through the night until he came into a neighbouring kingdom.

Dawn was just breaking when they reached the capital city. People there were surprised to see a young prince uttering strange cries and riding on a hyena. Just in front of the king's palace Shi-Guday lost his grip and fell off, and the hyena ran back into the forest. Men came and picked up the prince and dusted his coat respectfully.

'Why all this fuss?' said Shi-Guday. 'Haven't you ever seen a man riding a hyena before? Me, I prefer a lion, but my favourite mount went lame yesterday, so I had to be satisfied with that shabby beast.'

Among those who had watched the prince's arrival was the king's only daughter. The princess was no fool. She saw at once that Shi-Guday was putting on a show of courage, although he was really half-dead with fright. She also noticed that he was a handsome young man with a royal air about him. Already she was more than a little in love.

She went to Shi-Guday and said: 'Come. I will take you to my father. There is nothing he likes better than bravery in a man. You must let him hear that stirring war-cry "Ooer" and tell him about the lion you usually ride.'

The prince took her advice and made up a

convincing story about his bravery and daring. The king was impressed, especially when he discovered that this was the heir to the next kingdom. Here, he thought, was a good match for his daughter. So he made the young man welcome, and readily agreed when the two young people told him of their wish to marry.

The day chosen for the wedding was drawing near when news came that the country was being troubled by a great lion. Not content to slaughter sheep and cattle, the beast had taken to strolling into villages and helping itself to the fattest children.

'What luck that you should be here, my son,' said the king to Shi-Guday. 'My people are a peace-loving lot. They know nothing of lion-hunting. But you—why, this great brute will give you no trouble at all. Go after it with my blessing, and come back in triumph to your bride.'

Shi-Guday did not reply. His terror left him dumb. The princess knew just what he was feeling and what he needed to cure his fright. She gave him a big jar of strong drink, and when he had got this liquid courage inside him she loaded a horse with a fresh supply of the stuff. Shi-Guday clambered onto the horse and rode away, too confused in his head to know what he was doing, and all the people marvelled at his bravery as they cheered him on his way.

On rode the prince, singing a little song to himself. After a while the drink began to make him feel very sleepy. He hung onto his horse as long as he could, but at last he could go no farther. His grip loosened and he fell gently to the ground, where he curled up and fell fast asleep. The horse was alarmed and reared up, throwing the jar to the ground where it broke. All the drink flowed into a rocky hollow.

Towards midnight the lion came through the forest. The air was filled with the smell of strong drink. The lion sniffed and liked what he smelt. He took a long deep drink from the pool. It was good. He went on drinking until none was left. He came over weary and went fast asleep.

It was still dark when Shi-Guday awoke. His head ached and his eyes were blurred with the drink. He staggered to his feet, saw the lion lying beside him, and thought it was his horse. He scrambled onto the great beast's back. At this the lion woke up, just as muddle-headed as the man, and started to run, blundering into trees and roaring all the time. The prince realized what he had done. He clung tightly to the lion's mane and rode along, screaming 'Ooer ooer!'

That is how Shi-Guday returned to the city, riding a lion and uttering his war-cry. By the time they reached the palace the lion had had enough. The fumes of drink flooded his brain and he collapsed unconscious. Men ran with nets and entangled the mighty animal in them, while everyone gathered round the prince, cheering wildly.

'Well done,' said the king.

'It was nothing,' said Shi-Guday. 'I suppose I should have killed the lion, but my horse had run

away, so it seemed best to ride him home. He made a poor, spiritless mount though.'

The wedding was held with no more delay. Everyone was very merry, and none more than the prince who loved his bride dearly.

Happiness like that is too good to last long. A warlike tribe to the south suddenly invaded the country. Villages went up in flames and cattle and sheep were stolen.

The king sent for Shi-Guday.

'Dear son,' he said, 'this is your hour. My soldiers are made of poor stuff, but with you to lead them they will be filled to the brim with daring. Go with my blessing.'

They brought the prince a great war-horse. It towered above him, and what with its fierce snorting and its wild eyes he was scared almost to death. The princess saw what a state he was in, so she called two of her servants and got them to lift him into the saddle. Then they put ropes around his legs and tied them tightly under the horse so that he could not fall off. They pointed the horse in the direction of the enemy and gave it a prod with a spear.

Off shot the horse straight for the invading army. The soldiers followed, greatly heartened by the cries of 'Ooer ooer!' that came from their leader. They took up the cry and raced forward, waving their weapons and shouting 'Ooer ooer!'

Shi-Guday was in a panic. He couldn't stop his horse or control it. Seeing a small tree in his path, he grabbed it in the hope of checking his headlong charge, but the tree came up by the roots and the horse still ran on. He tried again and again, but each time he was left with a tree in his hands.

The enemy watched and wondered. Who could he be, this hero who thundered towards them on his great horse, tearing up trees by the roots as he came? As for the cries of 'Ooer ooer!' they filled the savage warriors with dread. Those in the front rank lost heart, threw away their spears, and ran, and the panic spread through the army. The battle was won before a blow could be struck.

Shi-Guday rode home in triumph. Never again was he called upon to fight a battle. When the old king died, the people made him their ruler, and whenever danger threatened Shi-Guday hired warriors to fight for him. There was no more need for him to prove his courage, and it seemed best to stay safely at home. Besides, his people could not afford to risk losing so brave a king.

SPAIN

# A REMARKABLE FIDDLE

I HAVE never been able to find out who made that fiddle but it surely was remarkable. It could make fine music, but it could make real trouble for its owner too, as you will see.

It all began when a stupid Italian servant signed up to work for a gentleman for three years. The fellow worked hard enough. He was honest too, which is more than you could say for his master. When the three years were up this fine gentlemanly scoundrel, who had bullied the poor man every day without mercy, paid him three pounds instead of the nine he had agreed to.

Poor Andrew didn't argue. He'd never had any money of his own before, and those three golden coins were wealth such as he had never dreamed of. He put his riches into his pocket and started for home.

He was striding along, singing at the top of his voice, when he heard a squeaky noise behind him. He looked round, and there stood a curious little fellow, barely half his own height and with the most devilish face on him. The dwarf was out of breath with running, but he managed to pant out: 'What makes you so cheerful?'

'Why wouldn't I be cheerful? I have got three whole pounds and all the world to spend them on.'

'True, there's nothing like money,' said the dwarf with a sigh. 'Me, I could do with some. I never had any money myself, only magic. See here, I'll do a trade with you; your money for my magic, or at least some of it. What do you say to three wishes for three pounds?'

'I'll think about it,' and Andrew did, with the whole of his great brain for about two minutes. Then he said: 'Agreed. I'll have your three wishes: one—a bow with arrows that always hit their mark, two—a fiddle that makes everyone dance, three—anything else I want whenever I want it.'

'They are yours,' said the dwarf. Andrew handed over his money, and at his feet appeared a bow and a quiver of arrows and a fine fiddle. The third wish, you see, was one that Andrew couldn't see, but he had it all the same.

The dwarf skipped away and Andrew continued his journey. He was happier than ever. He sang:

> *'No money*
> *That's no matter.*
> *Money will come*
> *And then I'll grow fatter.'*

It came sooner than he expected. He turned a corner and there in his path was a big fat money-lender. This lovely man was gazing at a tree in which a thrush was perched, singing most beautifully.

'What a voice!' said the money-lender. 'I'd give a lot to have a bird like that.'

'Nothing easier,' said Andrew, and he shot an arrow, and the bird dropped to the ground. The money-lender bent to pick it up. He looked so clumsy and ugly that Andrew thought he would have a little fun. He tucked his fiddle under his chin and started to play a jig. At once the fat money-lender began to dance. He kicked up his legs and turned somersaults, even though the dance led him through brambles and nettles until he was scratched and stung most piteously.

He could not endure it for long. 'For pity's sake, stop,' he said. 'You and that wretched fiddle are killing me.'

'What's it worth if I stop?'

'I'll give you a hundred pounds. It's all I've got on me,' said the unfortunate fat man.

So Andrew stopped playing and collected his earnings. Now he was rich indeed and happy enough for a dozen.

But the money-lender had gone straight to a magistrate and complained that Andrew had robbed him of a hundred pounds. So Merry Andrew was arrested, and there in his pocket was the money. He could give no excuse, so the judge found him guilty and condemned him to hang.

As he stood under the gallows the judge asked him if he had one last request. 'Yes,' said Andrew. 'I'd like to play just one more tune on my old fiddle.'

'Stop him,' shouted the money-lender.

'Nonsense,' said the judge. 'It's a small favour to give a doomed man. Besides, I like a good tune. Play away, my man, and make it something cheerful.'

'Oh,' said Andrew, 'it will be cheerful enough,' and he began his favourite jig. In no time everyone from the judge to the smallest errand boy was hopping around like madmen.

After a while the judge felt that he had danced enough for one day. 'That will do,' he cried. 'Stop playing now and let us get on with the hanging.'

'Don't be in such a hurry,' said Andrew. 'There will be time for hanging after the money-lender has told the truth.'

'What I said was the truth,' gasped the money-lender. But after another half-hour of dancing he was ready to sing a different tune, and with what little breath he had left he told how Andrew had won the money from him.

Then Andrew stopped playing and they all fell to the ground, panting and wheezing. When he got his breath back the judge said: 'Seeing we have the gallows all ready, I suppose we might as well hang the money-lender.' Everyone thought that was a good idea, specially Andrew.

So that was that.

There is not much more to say about Andrew, who went on playing his fiddle so successfully that he died a rich man. A music-seller bought the fiddle then, knowing only that it was a good instrument and not that there was magic in it. He sold it to a famous fiddler called Cabrera. This man was a fine musician but an ill-tempered fellow and more than a little jealous of his fellow players. It was not long before this began to have an effect on the fiddle.

There was, for instance, the concert in Madrid when the first performer, a young and unknown violinist, was a great success. Cabrera was furious. He went onto the stage determined to play this young upstart into the floor. But at the first touch of his bow, all four fiddle strings broke. He did look a fool! It took him a long time to fit new strings, so they called the young player back to keep the crowd happy. At last Cabrera was ready again. This time the fiddle started making dreadful wailing sounds; then it decided to play its jig. This set the crowd dancing, and before long they had all danced out of the hall, leaving Cabrera all by himself on the stage.

After that Cabrera got a bad name and no one wanted to come and pay to hear him play. In the end he died poor, and his fiddle came up for sale again. This time the price was low, and a young musician bought it. He was a nice young fellow, and for him the fiddle was prepared to make some beautiful sounds. Even so it had not lost its taste for stirring up trouble.

The young man had lodgings in the city in a big house where many other people were living. One day he was practising in his room when the fiddle took it into its head to play the jig, and of course everyone in the house had to dance. His fellow lodgers did not care for this, so they made a fuss and the landlord had to turn him out. The same thing happened wherever he went to live. Nothing would cure that fiddle of its tricks. In the end it even gave up waiting for its owner to play it; it took to playing itself all night long, and everyone within hearing just had to dance.

One day the young fiddler had suffered more than usual. He took himself to bed in a bad mood and was thankful to get to sleep. In the night he awoke feeling a weight on his legs. He lit a candle and saw what looked like a dwarf sitting on the bed. He blinked and looked again, and saw it was the fiddle lying there. He got up and put it back in its corner, laughing at his fancy.

When he woke up in the morning he glanced towards the corner and saw the dwarf again. He got up boldly and went over to it, and there, it was only his fiddle.

'This is queer,' he said. 'Either the fiddle is bewitched or I am going off my head.' He asked the priest's advice, and that good man came bringing holy water with him. He said a prayer and splashed holy water on the fiddle. There was a blinding flash of light, all the strings of the fiddle screeched together, and the instrument burst into ten thousand splinters. So that put an end to its tricks.

A ROMANY TALE

# A MAN OF STONE

THE KING's son walked in the marketplace. A holy beggar out of the desert was there offering a picture for sale. It was of a girl. The king's son saw it. He fell in love. He bought the picture, and set it up where all might see, offering a reward to anyone who could tell who the girl might be.

A ship came into port. The crew came ashore, heading for the inn. They passed the picture. 'That one's a beauty,' said the captain. One of his men—they called him Baldhead—looked and said: 'That is the dervish's daughter. What's she doing here?'

Soldiers grabbed him and took him to the king. 'What do you know of this girl?'

'I grew up with her.'

'Can you find her?'

'Yes. Give me a ship, a band of musicians too, and let the king's son come with me. And whatever I do, my word is law.'

'It is agreed.'


They sailed. Baldhead found land near the maiden's house. It stood on the cliff. He said: 'Hide yourselves. Let no man be seen.' Then he marched up and down the deck.

It was dawn. The sun shone on him. The maiden awoke and looked out of her window. She saw the ship. She saw Baldhead. She knew him. She sent a servant to bring him to her.

'Why are you here?'

'I came to see you. It is a long time since we were children together. Come. I will show you my ship.'

She went to make herself ready. Baldhead said to the crew: 'Keep hidden. When she goes to the cabin, up anchor and away.'

So she came to the ship, and they sat in the cabin, talking of old days. 'I must not stay long,' said the maiden.

'The day is young. Have some sweets.'

They ate. Again she said: 'I must go.' He sent for the musicians who played sweetly. The king's son came and bowed to her.

112

'Now I will go.' She went on deck. The ship went swiftly; the land was far away.

'You have tricked me.' She wept. The king's son comforted her.

'I love you. Rule my kingdom with me.' She wept no more.

The king's son takes her to the cabin. They eat and drink. Baldhead stays on deck. He steers the ship.

It is dawn. Three birds come to the masthead. He hears their singing and understands their words. One says: 'Pity the maiden and the king's son. They know not their fate.'

Another says: 'What will happen?'

'When they come to land a small boat will row out to bring them home. Then this boat will turn over and they will be drowned.'

The third bird says: 'If any hears this and repeats, he will be turned to stone up to the knees.'

Baldhead stands listening.

Next day at dawn the birds are there again. 'Pity the maiden and the king's son. Their fate is hard.'

'What will happen to them?'

'As they enter the city gate it will fall and crush them.'

'And if any hears this and repeats it, he will be turned to stone up to the waist.'

Still Baldhead listens.

At dawn on the third day the birds return. 'Pity the maiden and the king's son. They are doomed.'

'What will be their fate?'

'On their wedding night a dragon will come and eat them up.'

'And if any hears and repeats this, he will be turned to stone up to the head.'

Baldhead steers the ship into harbour. A small boat comes to take off the maiden and the king's son. 'Keep off,' shouts Baldhead. He steers for the shore. 'He will run aground,' shouts everyone. He does.

Baldhead takes them ashore. 'My word is law,' he says. They come to the gate. 'Pull it down,' says Baldhead.

'We will not,' they say.

'My word is law.'

They pull down the gate, and the maiden and the king's son go to the palace.

They hold the wedding. Baldhead says: 'I will sleep in the bridal room tonight.'

'You cannot,' they say.

'My word is law.'

Baldhead takes his sword and lies across the doorway. At midnight the dragon comes. Baldhead fights it and cuts off its head. He hides the head. The noise awakens the king's son. He sees Baldhead with sword drawn and he cries out in fear. The king comes, and his son says: 'Baldhead would have killed me. Bind him.'

In the morning they bring Baldhead before the king. 'You would have killed my son. Why should I not kill you?'

'Let me have three words with you.'

'Speak then, before your head leaves your body.'

'As I stood on deck, and your son and the maiden drank and made merry below, I heard birds speaking. They said that the bridal pair would drown in a small boat. If any heard this and spoke of it he would turn to stone up to the knees.'

And Baldhead turned to stone to the knees.

The king said: 'No more, boy. You have told enough.'

Baldhead went on: 'As they passed through the city gate it would fall on them and crush them. And if any heard this and spoke of it he would turn to stone up to the waist.'

And Baldhead turned to stone to the waist.

He went on: 'Then on the bridal night a dragon would come and eat them up. But I was there. Here lies the dragon's head and here the sword that killed it.'

And Baldhead said no more, for he had turned to stone even to the top of his head. Then the king and his son and everyone wept for him. They took his stone body and set it up as a memorial.

The king's son said: 'He died for me. Shall I not give my life for him?' He walked out into the world seeking his friend's salvation.


He walked and he walked, year by year. At last he came to a spring at the end of the world and drank. Then he lay down and slept. He dreamed. In his dream Baldhead came to him and said: 'A little earth from beside the spring will serve. Sprinkle it on the stone.'

The king's son took the earth and walked home. He went where the stone man stood and scattered soil over him.

Baldhead stretched his arms and said: 'I have slept long.'

They embrace. Together they go to the palace. Long lives Baldhead to serve the king's son.

MADAGASCAR

# THREE SISTERS

I T ALL happened because of Ifara's dream.
The three sisters lived together as happily as families usually do. But one night the youngest girl, Ifara, had a dream. In the morning she said: 'You'll never guess what I dreamed last night. Such a dream! The sun came down out of heaven to look for a wife, and what do you think? He chose me and left you two behind. Oh, handsome he was and kind with it.'

Her sisters were not pleased. They said to one another: 'The cheek of the child.

Sure, we know she is a pretty little thing in her way, but we are not all that ugly. Some people would say we are just as good-looking as she is.'

They took Ifara for a walk. Along the way they met an old woman, and they said to her: 'Hallo, Granny. Will you settle an argument for us? We can't decide which is the prettiest of us.'

'You are all nice girls, I'm sure,' said the old woman, 'but there is no doubt about it. The little one in the red dress is by far the prettiest.'

'It was a waste of breath asking her,' said the girls. So they made Ifara take off her pretty dress.

Soon they came upon an old man. 'Hey there, Grandpa,' they said. 'Did you ever see three such fine girls? Which do you think is the prettiest?'

'No doubt about that,' said the old man. 'You are bonny enough, but the little lass without a dress far outshines the sun.'

'Ifara is too pretty for her own good,' said the sisters. And they took away the rest of her clothes, so that she had to continue the walk all bare.

Next they came upon Itrimobe. My word, he was an ugly one. He had long fangs sticking out of his mouth, black hair all over his body, and a tail like a sharp sword. 'It's a fine day, Itrimobe,' said the girls, trembling with fear, for he looked hungry enough to eat all three of them. 'Which do you think is the prettiest of us?'

'Don't waste my time,' snarled the monster. 'The little naked one of course.' And he went away, lashing his tail and cutting down trees right and left with it.

119

Weren't those sisters angry? They said to one another: 'We shall just have to get rid of her. We dare not kill her ourselves, or mother and father would punish us. Let us make Itrimobe do it.'

They said to Ifara: 'We're going to pick some food for our dinner. Are you coming?' Then they went to Itrimobe's garden. The sisters picked close to the road, but they sent Ifara into the garden near to the monster's den. Sure enough, out came Itrimobe and caught her, while her sisters ran away.

'Now I've got you, you thief,' roared Itrimobe. 'I'm going to eat you.'

'Don't do that,' she said. 'I'm too skinny. I wouldn't make half a meal for a big strong fellow like you. Listen, I've got a better idea. I'll marry you and cook for you and keep your house clean.'

'Come on then,' said Itrimobe. (But he meant to fatten her up and then eat her.)

The parents were sad when the two sisters came home and told them that Ifara had been eaten by a monster. Meanwhile, Itrimobe fed Ifara well so that she began to get fat. But one day, when he was out hunting, a little mouse jumped into her lap and squeaked: 'Let me give you some advice.'

'I don't need advice from a mouse.'

'Very well,' said the mouse, offended. 'Just you wait and Itrimobe will eat you up.'

'I'm sorry,' said Ifara. 'Here, have some of this rice and tell me what to do.'

'Run away just as fast as you can,' said the mouse. 'And take with you a broom, an egg, a cane, and a round pebble.'

So that is what Ifara did. But first she pulled up a fat juicy young plantain from the garden and laid it in her bed, and she wrapped a sleeping-mat round it.

Soon Itrimobe comes home. It's time to eat Ifara and he has brought a cooking pot with him. He picks up his spear and goes to the bed. 'Good,' he says. 'She's sleeping and won't know what hit her.' So he sticks his spear through the mat. It goes into the plantain so hard that he can't pull it out. 'My!' he says. 'She *has* got fat.' He gives a strong heave and gets the spear out and licks the blade. 'That's funny,' he says. 'Her blood tastes of nothing at all. It must be all that fat.' He rolls back the mat. No Ifara! Just a plantain!

Itrimobe put his long hunter's nose into the air and sniffed deeply. Nothing to the north. Sniff. Nothing to the south. Sniff. Nothing to the east. Sniff, sniff. 'There she goes.'

When Itrimobe goes hunting, he can run like the wind. Soon he came upon Ifara. 'Now I've got you.' But Ifara threw down the broom and it became a dense thicket of thorn bushes. Itrimobe swung his long sharp tail, and cut through all the thorns in no time.

'I've got you, you bad girl.' Ifara threw down the egg and it became a big lake right across the path. Itrimobe lapped up the water like ten thousand thirsty cats, and he lapped it up until there was not one drop left.

'I've got you now.' Ifara stuck the cane into the ground, and at once it was a big forest of mighty trees. Itrimobe got to work with his tail and the trees fell like reeds.

'I've got you this time, little Ifara.' Ifara dropped the round stone, and it became a tall cliff with Itrimobe at the foot. He tried to climb it and slipped backwards. Then he swung his great tail, but the stone was too hard and it became more and more blunt with every stroke. He had to give up. 'Help me, little wife,' he called. 'I've been kind to you and fed you well. Now just lean over and pull me up.'

Ifara said: 'I don't care for the look of that sharp spear of yours. Stick it in the ground, and then I'll pull you up.'

Then Itrimobe stuck his spear into the ground so that the blade pointed to the sky. Ifara threw him down a rope, and he began to climb. He was nearly up to the top. 'I've got you, Ifara, my fat little wife.' She let go the rope, and he fell. Oh, what a sharp spear!

So Itrimobe was dead. Ifara wasted no time, but ran home as fast as her little legs could take her. Wasn't that a happy day for her father and mother? And if the sisters were not too pleased to see her again there was little they could do about it, so they were content to join in the rejoicing. All the neighbours were invited to a great feast of celebration. I was there, and ate so much that I couldn't go to work for a week afterwards. But Ifara was fat enough already. She ate just a little, and waited for the sun to come down and claim her for his bride.

CHINA

# THE NOSE

THE widow had two sons. They had fallen on hard times and scarcely knew where to look for their next meal. The poor widow would often break into tears, saying: 'Can't you find some work which will bring in a little money? Just look at that neighbour of ours; he is rich and has everything he could want while we starve. Why can't you be like him?'

The elder son said: 'Perhaps, as he's so wealthy, our neighbour will lend us a little money and then we can start a business of our own. I will ask him.' So he went to the neighbour, and by his honest looks and his sensible words he persuaded the good and very rich man to lend him a hundred pounds.

Then he said: 'This is what we will do. We will set aside ten pounds for mother to live on while we are away. Then you, brother, and I will take the rest. We will use ten pounds to pay our expenses until we get started, and that will leave eighty pounds to put into our business.'

Next day the brothers packed up for their journey. All their spare clothing and other things were put into one bag. Into the other went the eighty pounds. The elder brother slung the money-bag over his shoulder, while the younger carried the goods.

They walked for a few miles, and then the younger said: 'I bet that money-bag is heavy. How about changing loads for a bit to give you a rest?'

'That's all right,' said the other. 'I'll carry it for a few more miles.'

Well, they went on, and after a while the younger started again: 'Come on, brother. You must be worn out. Let me have the heavy bag for an hour or so.'

'That is good of you,' said the elder brother. 'But tell me at once if you get tired.'

So they changed over bags and walked on again. They had gone barely a mile when the younger brother began to groan. Then he dropped on his knees and crumpled up, holding his belly. 'Oh, the pain!' he gasped. 'My stomach is bursting. I must be ill. Run to the village and get me some hot soup, quick.'

The elder brother was greatly troubled. He ran off as fast as he could. As soon as he was out of sight the younger brother jumped up, grabbed the money-bag, and set off briskly in the other direction.

When the elder brother came back and could not find him he was more than ever distressed. 'Where can he have gone?' he said to himself. 'Perhaps he is better and has gone on his way, knowing that I can soon catch up with him.' So he shouldered his bag and went on his way.

When evening came he began to look for a place to shelter for the night. He came upon the ruins of what must once have been a beautiful palace with a big open hall. Here he made a bed for himself in a corner and soon got to sleep.

In the night he woke up hearing voices. Now this palace had been built not by humans but by the Gods themselves, and at night they came there to feast and talk. A voice said: 'Where is our food, Immortal Brother?' and another replied: 'Don't worry. I have only to tap with my wand and it will come, as much as you can eat and more.' And suddenly there was the most delicious smell of hot food. The Gods set to and ate a mighty meal. Then they sat back and began to talk.

'I wonder what is wrong with that spring over to the east,' said one voice. 'No one will drink from it, yet it sparkles clearly enough.'

'It is perfectly simple,' said another. 'A snake

has made its nest under the tree at the water's edge and it has poisoned the water. You need only cut down the tree and kill the snake, and it will become pure.'

'Human problems are always simple,' said another voice. 'Look at that new bridge to the west. They have been working on that for months, and they are no nearer completing it.'

'Yes,' said the first voice. 'All they have to do is dig deeper for the foundations and they will come on a hoard of gold and a hoard of silver. Take them away and the foundations will stand firm. Then the job can be finished.'

At this point the elder brother was overtaken by sleep and he heard no more. When he awoke it was dawn. The birds were singing and the sun shone, and of the Gods and their feast there was no sign. But when the brother looked around the hall he noticed a stick lying on a chair. Could it be the magic wand? He picked it up and tapped the table gently. At once the table was laid with rich food and drink. He ate a good breakfast, happy in his good fortune but sad that his younger brother was not there to share it.

He continued his journey. In the heat of midday he became thirsty. There was a woman washing clothes at a spring, and he asked her for a drink. 'You can't drink this,' she said. 'The water is bitter and it will make you ill.'

'Get your husband to cut down that tree,' he said, 'and he will find a snake in a hole underneath it. Kill the snake and you will have no more trouble.'

127

She thanked him and asked him what his name was.

So he went on his way. The road turned to the west, and in a few miles he came upon a gang of workmen building a bridge. They seemed to be having difficulties. 'What's the trouble?' he said. They said: 'It's these foundations. Just as soon as we get the footway into place the whole thing collapses.'

He went to the foreman and said: 'If I were you I'd dig that foundation a little deeper. You will find a hole there with a hoard of gold and a hoard of silver in it. Take them out and fill the gap with stones and you should have no more trouble.' The foreman was very grateful and asked the young man his name.

It seemed to the man that it was no use going any further. Without the money, which had vanished along with his younger brother, he could not hope to set up in business. So he went home. His mother wept with joy at seeing him, and with sorrow when he told her how his brother had been lost and the money with him.

'There is one piece of good come out of all this,' he said, and he showed her the wand. Then he struck the table, and it was covered with food. At least they would never go hungry again.

The news of the spring that was no longer poisoned and the bridge that could be built spread quickly, and at last it came to the ears of the Emperor. He made inquiries and discovered that one man had been responsible for both these improvements. He gave orders, and so the young man received a very large reward in silver and gold.

There was an end to his troubles. He was able to build a fine house and moved his old mother into it. Then he married a wife, and with her he lived in great happiness. Only the memory of his younger brother troubled him. If only he were there to share in the good fortune!

One day he noticed a beggar passing the house, dressed in rags and looking in need of a good meal. Suddenly he realized that this was his younger brother, grown old and worn with misery. He ran out of the house and embraced him. Then he brought him in and made much of him.

'You have done well for yourself,' said the younger brother bitterly.

'Yes,' he said, 'but it wasn't in business. Nothing came of that idea, after you and the money were stolen away.' And soon he was telling his brother the whole story.

'That's for me,' said the younger brother to himself when he heard about the hall of the Gods. As soon as he could get away he left his brother and hurried to the ruined palace. He lay down in a corner and waited for the Gods to appear. Soon he heard an angry voice saying: 'We have had no feasting here since you lost your wand, brother.'

'Someone must have stolen it,' said another. 'I wonder if the thief is still here.' And the Gods got up and searched the hall. It did not take them long to find a man lying in the corner.

'Here he is. Here's the villain who stole my wand.' And they gave him a sound beating. After that they got him by the nose and they pulled it and pulled it until it was a foot long.

He limped home and told his brother what had happened. 'Don't fret,' said the elder brother. 'Perhaps the wand will help. I'll go back tomorrow night and see what I can find out.'

He went to the hall and lay there very quietly. The Gods came. 'I did enjoy it last night,' said one voice. 'It was a real pleasure beating that thief.' 'Yes,' said another, 'and what about that nose? That was a beauty, and he will have to go around with it for the rest of his life.' 'Unless he still has the wand,' said the third voice. 'He has only to tap his nose twelve times, and it will go back to normal.'

Wasn't the elder brother pleased? He ran home and told his younger brother what had to be done. 'I'll do the tapping,' he said. 'I know all about the wand now.' So he tapped once, twice, three times, and on to twelve times. At each tap the nose shrank a little. After the twelfth tap the younger brother felt his nose, and said: 'It's still too big. Give it another.'

'Better not,' said his brother.

'Go on. It's not enough. Just one more.'

So, reluctantly, the elder brother tapped a thirteenth time, and the nose disappeared into the younger brother's face, leaving a big hole.

So that was that.

INDIA

# THE MANGO CHILDREN

THERE was a merchant whose wife had no children of her own. This was a bitter grief to her. She tried to find joy in her sister's children—for she had many—but it was in vain. Every day her tears fell more heavily. At last she said to her husband: 'It is no good. I can no longer live without my own child. I will go and seek Shiva, and the Great God will have pity on me.'

'You are a fool, woman,' said her husband. 'Where will you go to find Shiva, and even if you find him how can you be sure he will help you? Be content.'

She closed her ears to him, for her mind was made up. So she went into the jungle and travelled for many days, leaving her own home far behind and passing through many strange lands.

In time she came to a great river where travellers waited for a boat to take them across. Among these were two women, a queen and a dancing girl. The merchant's wife got talking to them and discovered that they were on the same mission as herself; they were seeking for Shiva to ask him for a child. 'This is a good omen,' said the merchant's wife. 'Let us travel together. Perhaps Shiva will listen to three prayers more kindly than to one.'

So that is what they did. Their journey went on for many weeks and they suffered many hardships on the way. But one day they came to another river, and this was one not of water but of fire. At the sight the queen and the dancing girl threw themselves on the ground and gave themselves over to despair. 'This is the end of all our efforts,' they said. 'We can go no farther. It has all been wasted.'

'Be cheerful,' said the merchant's wife. 'Perhaps this river of fire is the God's test of our courage. We must find a way across.' But the others feared the flames. 'Go if you can,' they said, 'and if you find Shiva remember us when you make your own prayer.'

Then the merchant's wife stepped into the river, and the flames rose up all about her, and yet they did not burn. So she walked through unharmed and reached the other bank.

Here she met still more dangers in a wild land full of tigers and boars and great snakes. But she gazed at them all and thought: 'They can kill me but once. It were better to die here now than to go back without finding Shiva.' So she walked on, and the savage beasts all moved aside to let her pass.

In Heaven the Great God himself was looking down, watching her. He marvelled at her courage, and it seemed to him that she had endured enough. So he made a mango tree grow up right in her path, while he disguised himself as a holy beggar and went and sat cross-legged beside the tree. But she was so set upon her quest that she took no notice of the rich fruit hanging on the tree or of the man sitting beneath it.

He called to her: 'Woman, come here. Where are you going?'

She said, without a glance in his direction: 'I have no baksheesh for you today, fakir. Go back to your prayers and leave me alone.'

'Come here, I said.' But she went on. He stood up and went and blocked her path. As he did so he returned to his own shape so that he shone like the sun. She cried out and fell down, kissing the ground before his feet.

He raised her up and said again: 'Woman, where are you going?'

She said: 'Lord, I am looking for Shiva, to beg him to give me a child.'

'Look no farther,' he said. 'I am Shiva.'

He plucked a mango from the tree and gave it to

her. 'Eat this,' he said. 'When you get home you shall have your child.'

'Lord,' she said. 'I had two friends on my journey. They too wanted children, but they feared the river of fire. Will you not have pity on them too?'

'Not for their sakes, because they lost heart,' said Shiva, 'but for your sake. Share your mango with them.' And he vanished.

The merchant's wife returned through the wild places and the fiery river, and the queen and the dancing girl were still waiting. They greeted her joyfully, and she shared her fruit with them, giving the queen the juice and the dancing girl the sweet pulp, while she herself swallowed the big stone.

So they returned home, each to her own country, and in nine months time each had a baby. The queen had a little princess who was named Chandra Bai, which means Moon Lady, for she was very fair. The dancing girl had a daughter too, called Moulee, while the merchant's wife had a son. She named him Koila, which means Mango Stone.

They were all beautiful children, but the little princess was the loveliest and, of course, the most richly dressed. She had everything that money could buy, as well as something that no money could give her, for when she was born she had on a pair of finely made anklets of gold and rare stones, and these grew as she grew. The king was very proud of his daughter, and he sent for all the wise men in India to come and tell her fortune. Many came and promised the child wealth and health and happiness. The most famous of them all, a very old Brahmin, when he saw her, tore his hair, and cried: 'The child must be destroyed or she will destroy all the land with fire.'

'What nonsense!' said the king. 'You talk like a fool, old man.'

'Bring me some wool,' said the Brahmin, and when it was brought, 'Lay it on the baby.'

They did so, and at once the wool flared up and burnt to ashes.

'So,' said the Brahmin, 'will she treat your kingdom.'

The king and queen were greatly troubled. The king was for having the child killed right away, but his wife pleaded so hard and with such tears that he relented a little. The baby should not be killed outright, but she must be put in a box which would then be thrown into the river.

The queen had a box made of pure gold, studded with precious stones, and little Chandra Bai was laid in it, the lid was shut, and the box floated away downstream. At last it could no longer be seen, and the queen returned to her palace, weeping.

The box floated on until it reached the country where the merchant lived. The merchant happened to be standing on the bank when it came into sight. He called to a fisherman: 'Throw out your net and catch me that box.'

'I'm a busy man,' said the fisherman. 'What is there for me if I do what you ask?'

'You can have the box. I'll take what is inside,' said the merchant.

So the fisherman drew in the box. He was pleased to find that it was richly made. He pulled up the lid, and inside lay a pretty baby, finely dressed, and wearing a pair of beautiful anklets.

The merchant said: 'We have both done well, fisherman.' He held out his hands and the baby came smiling into them. He carried her home to his wife, who was nursing her young son. 'Look,' he said, 'I have found a daughter to go with our son. Take good care of her and when she grows up she shall marry him. What a pretty pair they will make.'

Time went by. Chandra and Koila were married, and a fine pair they made too, the handsomest and the most beautiful young people in the whole country. The merchant's wife died and her husband soon followed her.

But what about the third Mango Child, Moulee, the daughter of the dancing girl? She too grew into a beautiful young woman. Like all her tribe she danced well, and she had a lovely voice. As the family moved around people came from miles about to hear her singing. In time Moulee and the other dancing people came to the country where Chandra and Koila lived.

Koila was hunting in the jungle when he heard in the distance the sound of a girl's voice. He had never in his life heard anything half so wonderful. He tried to follow the sound, but the singer seemed to move away in front of him and he could get no nearer. After several days of travel he found himself in the camp where Moulee's people were staying.

He saw Moulee dancing and singing with crowds of admiring people round her.

Koila stood in the shadow of the jungle and watched. After the song the people ran to the singer, struggling to kiss her hands and her feet. Many of the men were pleading with her to marry them and stay in their village for ever.

Moulee was excited. She took a garland from her neck and cried out: 'Whoever this garland falls on—he I shall marry.' She threw it as hard as she could. It flew through the air and dropped around the neck of the waiting Koila. All the people rushed to him and dragged him into their circle. They shouted: 'Here he is. He won the garland. He must marry Moulee.'

'I can't marry anyone. I have a wife already.'

'Never mind that. You can't argue with fate. You have been chosen and you must marry Moulee.'

Then they poured out strong drink and made him drink it so that his head became muddled. Soon he scarcely knew his own name, and his wife and home he had quite forgotten. So he married Moulee and they were happy enough together.

Moulee's mother, the dancing girl who had gone to find Shiva those long years ago, thought little of her new son-in-law. He might be handsome, but he could neither sing nor dance and he did no work. She bore it for a while, then she said to him: 'Son, you are a fine young man, God knows, but you are no use to us. If you can't work, at least go and get us some money. If you don't we will throw you out of the tribe and you can say goodbye for ever to your pretty Moulee.'

'I have no money,' he said. Then he thought hard and at last he remembered that he had another home and another wife. He said: 'I have it. I know someone who has two very fine anklets. She will give me one, and you can sell it for a lot of money.'

He went back to Chandra. His wife was not pleased when he asked for her anklet to give to his second wife, and that a common dancing girl. 'Shame on you,' she said. 'You deserted me and married a dancing girl who is far below you, and now you expect me to give you my most precious possession. I won't.'

'Forgive me,' he said. 'They got me drunk and tricked me into marrying Moulee. I am sick of them all. If I give them money they will be satisfied, and then I can come home to you for ever. I love no one but you.'

'Very well,' she said. 'You may have the anklet, but you are not deserting me a second time. I am coming with you.' So they went on their travels together.

Moulee's people had moved on again, and they were now staying in the country ruled by Chandra's own father and mother who lived on, still grieving for the loss of their baby daughter.

So it was that Chandra and Koila came to the king's city. They had nowhere to stay, but an old woman took pity on them and allowed them to sleep in her house. In the morning Koila left his wife sleeping while he went into the city to sell the anklet.

Now it happened that the king had asked a jeweller in the town to mend a pair of bangles belonging to the queen. The jeweller had cleaned one of them and left it on the window-sill to dry. An eagle flying by had seen it flashing in the sun and had stolen it. The jeweller was in a panic, for he knew that the king would be angry and that he must pay for his carelessness with his life. He went to the market to see if there was a good bangle for sale which he might hope to pass off as the king's.

There sat Koila, handsomest of young men, with an anklet for sale which was as good as the king's or better. He was surrounded by people, all marvelling as much at the man's good looks as at his splendid jewel. But none of them could afford to buy, and he sat all day without finding a customer.

The jeweller watched from a distance. The anklet was just right, but he could never find enough money to pay what it was worth. He said to his wife: 'It's getting late. The young man will give up soon and go home. Go and ask him to supper. Tell him we may be able to do a deal with him. When we have him safely in the house I'll think up something.'

That is what she did, and Koila was pleased to go to supper with these friendly people. But while he was eating the jeweller sent for the police, and they came and arrested Koila for, as they said, stealing the king's bangle.

They dragged him in front of the king, and the

jeweller stood up and said that the young man had stolen the bangle while it was in his care and had been caught offering it for sale in the market. They sent for the queen. When she saw the anklet she cried out and said: 'That is not my bangle. That is my Chandra's anklet that she was born with. No human craftsman made such a jewel. Where is she, my baby? What have you done with her?' And she made such a fuss that everyone thought she had gone mad and would not listen to her.

The jeweller gave the rest of his evidence, and the king judged that Koila was guilty of theft. He was condemned to death.

The soldiers took him out of the city. They would have cut off his head, but he begged them: 'Let me die by my own hand.' So he took his sword and he fell upon it and died.

The news quickly spread, and the people were angry that so fine a young man should have been killed on such slight evidence. There was nearly a riot, and the king had to act quickly and sternly, forbidding anyone to speak of the affair.

Meanwhile Chandra had passed a bad night at the old woman's house, full of frightening dreams. She awoke sure that something terrible had happened. The old woman tried to calm her, and persuaded her to stay at home while she went to find out what had happened. What she heard sent her hurrying back to Chandra with the worst of news.

Chandra at once ran to the palace and burst into the room where the king—her father, although neither knew it—was sitting. She cried out: 'What have you done with my husband?'

Her voice rang through the palace. At the sound the jewel cupboard burst open, and Chandra's anklet rolled out and came to rest at her feet. The king and queen looked on helplessly as Chandra fell to the floor and began to tear her clothes and her hair. As she touched her hair it burst into flames. The fire raced through the palace, destroying the king and the queen and all their court. Then it spread across the city, burning everything as it went. Only the old woman's house was spared. The jeweller's house went up in flames, and so did the jeweller and his wife. Far out on the edge of the city the fire leapt the gap and turned to ashes the dancing people's camp and Moulee and her mother.

The flames died down at last. Chandra stood alone among the ruins of her father's palace. She turned and walked away, through the smoking streets and out of the city gate. At the place of execution she found Koila's body lying, its dreadful wound gaping. She flung herself on it, weeping most piteously, and cried to Heaven for Shiva to help her in her grief. Down from the sky floated a needle and thread. She picked them up and, pulling the lips of the wound together, she sewed it up. Then the Great God breathed his power into him, and life came back into Koila's body.

Chandra took his hand, and together they went back through the scorched land to their own country.

HUNGARY

# THREE WISHES

THERE was this man. He was as poor as a cartload of muck yet happy enough, for he had married the prettiest girl for miles around, and, oh, how they loved each other. Of course things didn't always go right, and then they would throw hard words—and sometimes harder things—at the other's head. That mcant nothing at all, and soon they would be kissing and cuddling again.

One night the wife decided it was time to get supper ready for her man. He had been at work all day and would be hungry, poor fellow. For sure she had not a scrap of food in the house nor any notion of how to set about getting any, but a good fire would do for a start. So she put a light to the sticks and soon had a cheerful fire going.

In came her husband and threw himself down by the fire. 'That's good,' he said, and they warmed themselves side by side, both quite content.

'Any news, wife?'

'Not a thing. I've seen no one since you left this morning. Has anything interesting come your way?'

'I was working away in the fields,' said the husband, 'and in the distance I saw something moving. It got nearer and—do you know?—it was a golden carriage, pulled by four black dogs. It wasn't much bigger than my arm, and there was a pretty young woman inside.'

'Go on,' said his wife. 'What a liar you are!'

'It's true as true. Well, the road is inches deep in mud there, and the carriage got stuck. The dogs did their best, but they just couldn't move it. As for the woman, I could see that she was wearing a fine silk dress and gold slippers, and she didn't at all fancy getting them in the mud.

'I was scared stiff, I don't mind telling you. For all I could tell she might be a fairy and she would ill-wish me if I gave her an excuse. I was just going to run away when she called out for help. She had such a soft voice, I just couldn't leave her there. So I lifted her and her coach and dogs out of the mud with one hand, and put them down in the dry.

'She said: "Thank you, my good man. You have helped me and I will help you. Are you married?" I said I was. "Are you rich?" I said I was not. "You shall be, if you so wish. Let your wife make three wishes. I will make them come true." Then she called to the dogs and away they went like there was a fiery dragon after them.'

'And you believed her! You are a great fool, husband.'

'Nay, I'm not so sure about that,' said the man. 'Just you think up something to wish.'

'Well,' said the wife with a laugh. 'Here's a fine fire wasting with nothing to cook on it. I wish for a big sausage.'

At that there was a mighty noise in the chimney, and down came a frying-pan with a sausage in it long enough to wrap twice around their house.

Weren't they delighted? They hugged one another and danced round the room for joy. 'But be careful, wife,' said the man. 'We must sit down and think this out carefully. We have two more wishes and we mustn't waste them.'

They sat together by the fire, thinking deeply. 'A herd of cows and some horses and a few pigs would be good,' said the man. 'With those we would be set up for ever after.'

He took out his pipe because he thought that a smoke would make his brain work faster. He tried to light it with a cinder from the fire, but, clumsy fellow, he managed to overturn the frying-pan and the great sausage fell into the fire.

'You are a stupid clumsy clown,' said his wife. 'I

wish that sausage was stuck on your nose.'

And of course it was.

'You look uglier than ever,' said the woman, and she burst out laughing.

'Never mind the jokes,' said the man. 'Get this thing off me.'

Well, she pulled, and he pulled, but that sausage was not to be shifted.

'Shall I try the carving knife?' she said.

'Just you dare!'

'Then you will just have to live with it.'

'There is one chance,' said the man. 'You have

147

wasted two wishes, but there is one left. Wish the sausage back in the pan and at least we can have our supper in peace.'

'What about all the cows and horses and pigs we might have had?' said the wife. 'We could have lived like lords with those.'

'It can't be helped. I'm not going round with a sausage on my nose for the rest of my days. Besides, you can't get near enough to kiss me.'

So the wife used up her last wish, and they sat down and ate that sausage, and very good it was too.

After that, somehow, they didn't quarrel half as much. This gave them more time for work and so they became quite wealthy, with all the cows and horses and pigs they might have wished for. So, in a way, they got their wishes as well as their supper.

YUGOSLAVIA

## APPLES OF GOLD

IN THE king's orchard grew a hundred apple trees. Ninety-nine bore fine apples which the king's sons ate. The hundredth tree stood bare all day, but in the evening it grew golden apples that ripened as darkness fell. Yet in the morning, strange to say, there was never an apple to be seen.

The king wondered at this. 'I would give much,' he said, 'to know where the golden apples go.'

'Give me a third of your kingdom and I will find out,' said the eldest son; and that night he went into the orchard to watch. But sleep came over him quickly, and when he awoke it was dawn and the apples were all gone.

'Give me a palace of crystal and I will keep watch,' said the second son. But when morning came he was still snoring, and on the tree not one apple waited to be plucked.

'Give me your blessing,' said the youngest son. He went to the orchard while the sun was still high, made himself comfortable and was soon asleep. He woke up promptly at midnight. It was lighter than day in the orchard because the golden apples were glowing brightly. There was a sudden noise of wings and nine peahens flew down. Eight of them settled in the tree. The ninth came to the ground beside him and at once turned into a most beautiful maiden, crowned and stately.

What were golden apples to the prince then? He took her in his arms and stayed happily with her until dawn. Then, as the first light came into the sky, the peahens prepared to fly away, taking the golden apples with them. The prince begged for a single apple as a keepsake, and the maiden gave him two, one for himself and one for the king. Then she put on her bird shape, and they all flew away.

The prince gave his father the two apples but said not a word about peahens or princesses. He went back to the orchard next night and the same thing happened. Now the older princes were becoming curious. They bribed their old nurse to follow their brother on the third night and see what

happened. She saw him sleeping and watched as the peahens flew into the tree and the ninth bird turned into a beautiful maiden. Quickly and quietly she took her scissors and cut a single lock from the maiden's long hair. At once the peahen princess uttered a loud call of distress and turned back into her bird shape, and she and the others flew away, each sending out her shrill sad cry. The prince awoke just in time to see them flying off.

The golden apples still hung on the tree, but the peahens never returned, although the prince watched every night for many weeks. He was heart-broken and nothing his father could do or say would cheer him. At last he decided that he must go out into the world and find his peahen, no matter where the journey might take him. He wandered far and wide, in forest and desert, bitter cold and great heat, but nowhere could he get news of the birds.

At last his travels led him to an old palace standing on the shores of a lake. A queen lived there with her only daughter.

'Where are you going, young prince?'

'I seek nine peahens.'

'You need search no more. They come here every day to bathe in the lake. But what do you want with them?'

The prince told her how the ninth peahen was a beautiful princess and that he was determined to marry her.

'Foolish young man, do you hope to find happiness with a bird? Why not take my daughter instead? See: she is lovely, and wealthy too. What more could you want?'

But he would not even look at the girl. Next day, as soon as the sun was up, he went down to the water's edge to wait for the peahens. But the queen had resolved that he must marry her daughter. She had slipped a drug into his wine, and very soon a great drowsiness came over him and he lay in the sun, deeply asleep.

At noon the peahens flew to the lake. The ninth bird turned at once into a beautiful maiden, who ran to the prince and took him in her arms. 'Awake, my love! Awake, my heart!' But he lay still as if he were dead and she could not rouse him. She dropped a single feather beside him and flew away with her sisters.

When the prince awoke the sun was setting, and he knew that he had missed his love. He was bitterly angry, but he could do nothing except pick up the feather and return to the palace.

The same thing happened next day. When the prince woke up from his drugged sleep he found two feathers lying over his heart but there were no birds to be seen.

A third time he went to the lake, but the queen had done her wicked work again, and he slept. The maiden kissed him and shook him, but he knew nothing of it. At last she gave up trying to wake him. She laid three feathers over his heart, and away she flew with her sisters, weeping sadly.

On the next morning the prince continued his journey, leaving the queen angry and her daughter unhappy. So he wandered on from kingdom to kingdom until at the very edge of the world he heard tales of a golden city ruled over by nine golden birds. He hurried on with hopeful heart until he saw the city shining in the distance.

The gates stood open and he rode in until he came to the palace. The queen of the city came running to meet him, and who was it but his own beloved peahen. What a meeting that was! The news travelled quickly through the streets, and very soon the whole city, including eight peahen princesses, gathered, cheering and singing joyfully, while the prince married his peahen queen.

They lived happily together in the palace for many days, and might have gone on living happily ever after. But one day the queen was called to meet the king of a neighbouring country, and the prince had to stay behind. Before she left the queen gave him the keys of the palace. 'Go where you like, my love, and be happy. But do not enter the deepest cellar or you will suffer for it.' So she rode away, and the prince was left alone.

He wandered contentedly through the halls and corridors of the palace, gazing at the fine paintings and picking up here a bowl of flowers, there a glass of wine, but always at the back of his mind he was wondering what could be hidden in the deepest cellar below the palace. In time he found himself standing outside the cellar door. He put out a hand and pushed the door, and it creaked open. Inside all was dark, but he could just see that the cellar was empty except for a spring of water that bubbled in

154

one corner and a big barrel standing upright, bound with three great hoops of iron.

A voice called out of the depth of the barrel: 'A drink, for the love of God. Give me water or I die.' Without thinking, the prince took water from the spring and poured it into the barrel. At once the lowest of the iron hoops burst with a loud noise. Again the voice called: 'More. Give me water or I die.' The prince took more water from the spring and poured it into the barrel. The middle hoop burst, and the voice called out: 'Still more. Water, for God's sake. More water.' A third time the prince went to the spring and took water to the barrel. There was a great bang, the last hoop burst, and the whole barrel fell in ruins. Out of it came a dragon. It knocked the prince head over heels and rushed from the palace.

Outside the city the queen was coming back from her mission when she met the dragon. It snatched her from her horse and hurried away with her. Her escort rode back to the palace and told the prince what had happened.

Once again the prince had to go on his travels in search of his queen. He wandered on through many lands, but nowhere could he get news of the dragon. One day he came to a lake. It had dried up at the edge, leaving a small fish stranded and dying for want of water. It called to him: 'Help me, brother. Throw me into the lake.'

The prince willingly did so. 'Bless you, brother,' said the fish. 'Here, take a scale from my side. If you need my help, rub it in your fingers and I will come.'

This the prince did, and went on his way. A day or two later he came upon a fox caught in a trap. It called out: 'Help me, brother. For God's sake open this cruel trap.'

The prince knelt down and pushed open the jaws of the trap, and the fox jumped clear. 'Bless you, brother,' it said. 'Take this hair from my tail. If you should need my help, rub it in your fingers and I will come.'

The prince travelled on. In the forest he came upon a wolf that had been crushed under a fallen tree. It called to him: 'Help me, brother, or this tree will squeeze the life out of me.'

The prince put out all his strength and managed to roll the tree away. Out crawled the wolf and shook itself. 'Bless you, brother,' it said. 'Take a hair from my neck. If you need me, rub it in your fingers and I will come.'

At last, after many months of wandering, the prince came upon a palace standing alone in the wilderness, and there he found his queen again. The dragon was away from home, so they at once prepared to escape. They found a good horse in the stable, and they galloped away at the best speed they could manage.

Very soon the dragon came home. He was angry when he found that the queen had escaped, but his horse said: 'There's no hurry. Let us eat and drink, and we shall soon catch up with them.' So they ate a good meal, and then the dragon mounted his horse, and, sure enough, they quickly caught up with the runaways. The dragon snatched up the queen and tied her to his horse. To the prince he said: 'I ought to kill you for this, but I remember how you saved me from the barrel. Go in peace. If we meet again you will surely die.'

So he rode back to his palace, leaving the prince in despair. But after a while he took heart and crept back secretly. There sat the queen in tears. They kissed and talked for a long time, trying to plan a way to escape. The prince said: 'We must have a horse as swift as the dragon's. Question him, and find where he got his steed. I will be back to-morrow.'

When the dragon came home the queen spoke gently to him and served him a good meal. When he was well contented she said: 'Ah, my lord; what a fine horse that is of yours. Wherever did you get such a treasure?'

He said: 'Why, my love! In the mountains there lives an old woman who has the finest stable in the world. There you will find a dozen horses which have no match for beauty and strength. Yet they are nothing compared to the broken-backed old stallion that stands in a corner. That one may look like a hack, but he is the best horse in the world.'

'How could one get that horse?' asked the queen.

'That is not easy. If you wanted that horse you would have to serve the old woman for three days and nights, guarding the old woman's mare and foal. Succeed, and the horse is yours. But if you fail the old woman will have your head.'

All this the queen repeated to her prince next

day. So he went into the mountains and at last found the stable. 'God be with you this day, mother mine,' said the prince. 'Bless you, son,' said the old woman. 'What is it you want?'

'I would be your servant.'

'So you shall. Serve me well for three days and three nights, and you may choose a horse, whichever you please, from my stable. But if you fail me, I must have your head.' And she took him into the yard. There were many stakes sticking out from the walls, and on each was a head. But one stake had no head, and it cried out all the time: 'Give me my head.' The old woman said: 'Be patient. You shall have your head.'

She then set the prince to work. He was to take the mare and foal out to graze and guard them closely. So he mounted the mare and rode out to the paddock, and the foal followed its mother. He thought it would be safest to stay on the mare's back, but he became very weary and about midnight he dropped off to sleep. When he woke up it was dawn; the mare and foal had gone and he was sitting astride a fence holding the bridle in his hand.

In his mind he could hear the stake calling: 'Give me my head.' He was greatly afraid and looked everywhere for the mare. He came upon a little pond, and this put him in mind of the fish. He took out the scale and rubbed it in his fingers. At once the fish appeared, and he explained his problem. The fish said: 'The mare is in this pond, turned into a fish, and her foal too. Just lash the water with the bridle and call her, and she will come.'

He did this, and the mare and foal came out of the water. He mounted and rode the mare home. The old woman gave him food, but the mare she dragged to the stable and beat her sorely for allowing herself to be caught.

In the evening he rode out again with the mare and foal. Again he fell asleep in the saddle, and when he awoke the mare had gone. He hunted everywhere, and noticed a fox-hole in a little wood. At once he remembered the fox, and he took out the hair and rubbed it in his fingers. The fox came out of the hole, and the prince told him what had happened. 'The mare is down the hole,' said the fox. 'She has become a vixen, and her foal is a cub. Just strike the earth with the bridle and call her, and she will come.' And so it was.

Once more the prince got his meal and the mare her beating. When the third evening came the prince rode out again, but again he slept, and the mare disappeared. In the morning he looked for her, and in a dark corner of the forest he smelt the strong smell of a wolf. At once he took out the wolf's hair and rubbed it in his fingers. The wolf came bounding through the trees. 'What is your trouble, brother?' he asked. The prince told him what had happened. 'The mare is in my den, dressed as a she-wolf, and her foal is with her. Strike the tree with the bridle and she will come.' And that is what happened.

The prince rode back on the mare and the foal followed. The old woman gave him a fine meal, for he had completed his task, but to the mare she said: 'Faithless one, you have betrayed me. Why did you not hide among the wolves?'

'Forgive me, mother,' said the mare. 'Fish, fox, wolf, all these are this man's friends, and there's no hiding from him anywhere.'

'Well, mother,' said the prince. 'My work is done. May I take my pay and go?'

So the old woman took him into the stable where the twelve great horses tossed their heads and trumpeted with their great voices. 'Take your pick,' she said. 'Whichever one you want, it is yours.'

He looked about him and said: 'These horses are too grand for me. I will take that poor broken-backed stallion in the corner.'

'Don't be a fool. Take one of the good horses.'

'You promised that what I choose, that I shall have. The old horse is the one for me.'

The old woman could not make him change his mind, so he slipped a halter over the old horse's head and led it away. When he reached the shelter of the forest he took a brush and groomed the old horse until its coat shone like gold. He jumped on its back, and it ran as lightly and swiftly as a falcon. They very soon reached the dragon's palace. The queen was alone, and they quickly mounted the horse and rode away.

Very shortly the dragon came home. He saw that the queen had gone, and said to his horse: 'Well, what shall we do? Eat and drink and then catch the queen, or go after her without food?'

'It makes no difference. We shall never catch them.'

Then the dragon mounted his horse and galloped as fast as he could. The prince saw them coming and urged his horse to greater speed, but the horse said: 'There's no hurry.' It slowed down a little so that the dragon's horse could come closer. This one called out: 'Hold on! I'll kill myself if I keep up this pace, brother.'

'More fool you,' said the prince's horse. 'Why must you be a slave to that stupid blundering dragon? Kick up your heels and be rid of him.'

So the dragon's horse tossed his head and reared up, sending the dragon flying, and when he came down he broke every bone in his body. Then the dragon's horse trotted up to its brother. The queen mounted, and they all went back to their palace, where the queen and the prince and the two great horses spent their days in peace and great happiness.

JAPAN

## LITTLE WOODEN TOP

SHE WAS a lovely young girl. Indeed she might have been called the fairest in all Japan, but, as she lived in a remote cottage with only her parents for company, no one knew of her beauty.

Then her father died. Her mother too became feeble and feared that she must soon follow her husband to the under-world. What would happen to the lovely daughter then?

She called the girl, who came swiftly like some fragile butterfly.

'Dear child,' said the dying woman. 'I am troubled for you when I am gone; and that will not be long now. Your father and I have always kept you safe from the world. You must learn that there are those who would drag you down into the dust because of your beauty. If you are wise, you must hide your face. That way you will stay safe from evil men.'

She took up a wooden bowl, finely polished and painted, and put it on the young girl's head so that her face was quite hidden. 'There,' said the woman, 'wear this all the time and you will come to no harm.'

It was not long after this that the mother died and the girl was left all alone. She wept greatly for her lost parents, but, ah well! life had to go on. She found work in the rice fields. She was a good little worker, keeping at it while there was light in the sky, but everyone thought how strange it was that a young girl should wear a bowl on her head while she worked. Some of the workers threw rude words at her, and one or two of the young men would have snatched the bowl off, but they were prevented. Before long she was known to everyone as Little Wooden Top.

The farmer who owned the rice fields noticed Little Wooden Top. Her strange head-covering worried him not at all, for he saw how hard she worked and how neatly too, with never any waste. After a while he said to her: 'You work well. I like the way you never chatter and giggle with the other girls. You shall have work in my fields till the harvest is done.' And at this she was much relieved, because she needed the work in order to live.

The season passed and the rice was gathered in. The farmer sent for Little Wooden Top and said: 'Now that winter is coming, you will need some different work. My wife is ill and needs someone to look after her. Will you be her nurse?'

Of course Little Wooden Top was pleased. She made a good nurse too, always cheerful and clean. The sick woman grew fond of her, and she and the farmer were soon treating the girl as if she were their own daughter.

After a time the farmer's son came home. He had been living in the city where he was a student, although, to tell truth, he had spent more time feasting and drinking than reading his books. But the merry life had at last begun to turn sour, and he was glad to be home on the farm.

'Whoever is that funny girl with the wooden bowl on her head?' he asked his father. 'She seems very much at home here, but I've never seen anyone quite so odd.'

'That is our Little Wooden Top. She lives here because she has no father or mother. She is a dear girl and a good one, as you will soon see for yourself. I must admit that I wish she didn't wear that ugly bowl, but it is her wish and we must respect it.'

The young man soon settled into the life of the farm and enjoyed it greatly. Every day he became more enchanted with the queer little girl whose face was hidden by a bowl. He loved her cheerful ways and her willingness to help, and the way she sang at her work. In no time at all he found himself in love with her.

He told his friends. 'You must be mad,' they all said. 'You can't love a girl you've never seen. She may have the ugliest face in Japan. You don't know what you may be letting yourself in for.'

But whatever they said, he became more determined every day to marry her. At last he told her of his love. 'Will you marry me?' he said. She at once began to weep. 'You know I can never marry you,' she said. 'I am nothing but a servant in your parent's house. I am nothing and you are the master's son.' And no words of his would make her change her mind.

How sad she was! That night she cried and cried until she had no tears left. At last she slept, and in her dreams her dead mother came to her. 'Marry the lad,' she said. 'Everything will work out for the best, never fear.'

At that her heart was lightened. Next morning the son came to her again and begged her to marry him, and this time she agreed.

The time came for the wedding. 'We must get rid of that bowl,' said the farmer's wife. The girl tried to lift it off, but it would not budge. Some of the others tried, but the bowl made terrible groaning and screaming noises and nothing would shift it.

'It is no matter,' said the farmer's son. 'I love my Little Wooden Top, and I'll marry her, bowl and all.'

165

So the wedding took place. It was time for the bride and bridegroom to drink to each other. The bride put the cup to her lips. There was a big bang, and the bowl split from side to side. It tumbled to the ground, and out of it fell a shower of precious stones. All the guests looked in amazement at the bride and saw a woman of the most extraordinary beauty, the skirts of her dress littered with gold and jewels. As for the bridegroom, all he knew was that his Little Wooden Top was the rarest jewel in all Japan.

ARABIA

# THE DOCTOR'S REVENGE

THERE once lived a mighty king. His power stretched over all the land from sunrise to sunset. He was rich beyond a man's imagining, and he had no enemies, for his armies had never been defeated.

Yet one enemy crept upon him when no one was on guard. It was leprosy, a disease that rotted his body slowly and threatened to end his life.

At first he kept it a secret from all but his wives and his closest advisers. In time it could no longer be a secret because it was written in the king's face for all to see. Then he sent out messengers through the world offering rich rewards to anyone who could cure him of his dreadful sickness.

One day a wise and learned doctor came to the city and asked to see the king. His name was Rayyan. Where he came from no one knew, but he had studied all the sciences. He brought with him a library of books in all known languages and in some known only to himself, as well as great chests of herbs and other medicines.

Led before the king, he bowed low. 'Lord,' he said, 'I know what evil you are suffering. I will cure you, and I will do this without drugs or ointments or any of the trickery practised by others of my trade.'

'Can this be true?' said the king.

'Give yourself into my hands and you will suffer no pain or weariness.'

The king readily agreed, and the doctor chose the following day for the cure.

Rayyan went back to his lodgings and shut himself up with his medicines and his books. He chose certain secret drugs and mixed them over a slow fire. Then he sent out for wood and cane and wool, and out of these he made a polo mallet and a polo ball. The handle of the mallet was hollow, and into it he poured his medicines and sealed the end.

In the morning he went to the palace and bowed to the king. 'Lord,' he said, 'it is time for you to take some exercise. Your body will welcome a game of polo and you will be much better for it.'

And he led the way to the polo ground.

The king mounted his pony and took the mallet in his hand. Then he and his courtiers played a hard game in the hot morning sun. The king twisted and turned and struck the ball hard. By the end of the game he was soaked with sweat, and the heat of his hand had drawn the drugs out through the mallet handle and into his body.

When he came off the field the king had not felt so well for many years. He rode back to the palace in high spirits, took a bath, and went to bed. There he slept deeply for twenty-four hours. When he awoke he looked at himself in the mirror. The leprosy had left him.

The king sent at once for Rayyan. When the doctor entered the throne room the king walked to meet him and insisted that they should sit side by side on the throne. A great feast was served, and everyone rejoiced that the king was well again. Then Rayyan returned to his lodgings, laden with gold and treasure.

Again on the following day the king sent for Rayyan and did him great honour, and made all his court do the same. At the end of a long day of feasting and rejoicing the doctor went back carrying still greater gifts.

Now, among the ministers who had been closest to the king in the days of his sickness there was one, an old man, cunning and clever but filled to the brim with greed and jealousy. This man waited until he could speak secretly to the king. Then he said: 'Lord, I am deeply troubled for you.'

'Why so, old friend?' said the king. 'Surely you must rejoice with all the rest that I am cured of my sickness.'

'There are worse sicknesses than leprosy,' said the minister. 'One of them is death! I fear greatly that your life is in danger.'

'I have no enemies,' said the king proudly.

'Lord,' said the man; 'I have watched you heaping riches and honours on a man you know nothing of except that he is a master of some cunning tricks. This Rayyan is your enemy.'

'Rayyan is my friend,' said the king. 'He has done me a service when no other man could. I honour him for it and delight in giving him great riches. Half my kingdom would not be too much for a reward.'

'I fear that he may not be satisfied with half. He plans to kill you and seize the whole kingdom.'

'I cannot believe it,' said the king.

'How did he cure you?' said the old man. 'Through the palm of your hand on a polo mallet. Could he not as easily kill you in just such a way?'

For all his power the king had always gone in fear that someone might one day kill him, and he began to listen to the wicked one's words and to believe that they might be true. From that moment he watched Rayyan carefully, and every action that he made or word that he spoke seemed to threaten his safety. Very soon he was ready to believe that the doctor was only waiting for the right moment to strike him down.

'I won't wait for that,' said the king. 'I will strike first.' And he sent for Rayyan.

'Do you know why I have called you?' he said.

'Who can know your thoughts except God?' said the doctor calmly.

'I have sent for you that you may die.'

'Die? But what have I done?'

'You are a traitor and a spy. You planned my death, but I shall kill you first.' And the king sent for the executioner and said: 'Take off that traitor's head.'

'Mercy!' cried the doctor. 'For God's sake spare my life, or one day God will rise up and kill you.'

'There is no other way,' said the king. 'You must die or you will kill me. I dare not let you live.'

'So this is my reward,' said Rayyan. 'I saved you from a dreadful disease, and you repay me in this unjust way.'

Even the king's own guard murmured at this and said: 'He saved you, Lord. Will you not save him?'

'He must die,' said the king, and would have no more argument.

Then the doctor asked the king's leave to go once more to his lodgings to make some last arrangements and to fetch a book which he wished the king to have. So the king let him go under guard, and he returned carrying a small but very ancient book. He knelt for a moment with the book before him, muttering to himself. Then he said: 'Since I am to die, take this book and remember me. Do not open it until I am gone. Set my head on the table beside

you and read what the book has to say to the king
on the subject of gratitude.'

Then he bowed his head, and the executioner
took it off neatly. They put it up on the table, and
the king picked up the book eagerly. The first pages
seemed to be stuck together, so the king licked his
finger and turned them with some difficulty. It was
the same with the next pages, and the next. He
looked closely at them, getting all the while more
puzzled.

'What can the traitor mean?' he said. 'All these
pages are blank.'

He tried a few more, but they were all the same,
and all the time the doctor's head watched him
with open eyes.

Suddenly the king was seized with terrible pains. The poison that had been laid on the pages and which he had taken into his body when he licked his fingers worked swiftly. He fell down, gasping 'Treason! Treason!' and then the dead doctor's lips opened and said:

> 'Terrible is it
> when the wicked
> judge the good.
> More terrible
> when the good
> judge the wicked.'

He said no more, and in that instant the king died.

FRANCE

# CHEATING THE DEVIL

**J**EAN-PAUL had always fancied himself as a landowner, and though he was just a poor peasant he saved up his pennies until they became pounds and at last he had enough to buy a small farm. One came onto the market at the right time, and remarkably cheap it was too. So he put down his money and he and his pretty wife moved into the farmhouse.

Next morning he went into his fields. It felt good treading his own land with his big boots. But who is this fellow striding towards him? It was a tall man. He looked like a real gentleman in his fine clothes, but what were those things sticking out of his forehead? And wasn't there something queer about his feet? And surely there was a strong smell of sulphur in the air?

The gentleman said: 'Well, my lad; what are you going to plant for me this year?'

Jean-Paul said: 'I plant what I please in my own bit of land.'

'That won't do at all. If they sold you this field you were cheated. It has been mine for more years than you can count. Get this into your thick head; I'm the master here.'

Jean-Paul didn't like this one bit, nor did he like the man's looks and the angry way he was swishing his tail. So he said nothing.

The devil said: 'You look a likely lad. I'll tell you what we'll do. You work the land for me, and I'll go equal shares with you. How's that?'

'Right,' said Jean-Paul. 'Which half will you take, above or below ground?'

'Above,' said the devil.

So Jean-Paul set to work and he planted turnips. When they were ready he went out with his cart and the devil came too. Jean-Paul dug up the turnips, cut off the tops and gave them to the devil, and kept the turnips for himself. Then they went to market. Jean-Paul sold his turnips in no time, but the devil hadn't found a single buyer by nightfall.

'You tricked me,' said the devil angrily. 'But you won't get away with it twice. Next time I'll have what's under the ground.'

'Just as you say,' said Jean-Paul, and he planted wheat. When harvest time came around the devil was there waiting, and Jean-Paul gave him his share, a load of dry stubble. Once more they went to market, and Jean-Paul made a good profit while the devil got only jeers and a kick or two.

'You are a scoundrel,' he said to Jean-Paul. 'But you won't fool me a third time. Next year I'll have what's above and what's below. You can have what's left.'

So Jean-Paul planted runner beans. When the beans were ripe he picked them, and he let the devil have the stalks and roots for himself. They went to market, and by the end of the day the devil was raging fit to burst.

'I've had enough of this, you ruffian. We will settle the matter once and for all. Meet me tomorrow at dawn on Devil's Bridge, and we shall find who is master.'

'How is that?' asked Jean-Paul.

'We'll both come riding. If I can say what your beast is you will work for me for ever. If you can name mine I'll give you the farm—no argument.'

'Right you are,' said Jean-Paul.

Jean-Paul got up very early, while it was still dark. His wife got up too, and he made her strip. First he smeared her all over with honey. Then he tore open a feather bed, and she rolled in the feathers until they stuck to every part of her. She looked like some very strange, very big bird. He had a donkey's tail which he hung over her head so that it dangled in front, hiding her nose. Then he

178

put a saddle and bridle on her, and they walked together to Devil's Bridge.

As light began to appear in the sky they heard the devil coming from the other direction. He was talking to his horse: 'Gee up, Ricalon de Bigorne. Steady there, Ricalon de Bigorne.'

What a horse! As it came into sight Jean-Paul saw that it had long horns, furry feet and two tails. What else it had he missed because the devil had reached the bridge, and he had to be there to meet him. He climbed on his wife's back and rode onto the bridge.

They met in the middle.

'Hallo there,' said Jean-Paul. 'It's a beautiful morning.'

'Never mind that,' said the devil. 'What am I riding?'

'You are a simpleton and no mistake,' said Jean-Paul. 'Whatever made you pick such a common beast. Why, every school-kid knows that's a Ricalon de Bigorne.'

Wasn't the devil angry! He got down from his queer beast and walked around Jean-Paul and his steed. He sniffed and prodded it, but he could make nothing of so strange an animal.

'I give up,' he said at last. 'There just isn't any such beast. I don't believe my own eyes. You win, curse you. The farm is yours.'

And he jumped on his impossible horse and rode away, while Jean-Paul took his little wife home to wash off the feathers. They never saw him again.